S
U
Z
Y
S
U
Z
Y

BY THE SAME AUTHOR

Novels
Alice Falling
Minding Children
The Map of Tenderness
This is the Country
Grace's Day

Short Fiction
No Paradiso
Hearing Voices/Seeing Things
The Islands

Poetry
Mathematics & Other Poems
Fahrenheit Says Nothing To Me
Ghost Estate
The Yellow House

WILLIAM WALL

SUZY SUZY

First published by New Island Books, DAC,
16 Priory Office Park,
Stillorgan, Co. Dublin,
Ireland.

Head of Zeus Ltd
First Floor East
5–8 Hardwick Street
London EC1R 4RG
www.headofzeus.com

NEW ISLAND

HEAD of ZEUS

First published by New Island Books and Head of Zeus in 2019
This paperback edition published in the UK in 2019 by Head of Zeus Ltd

9 7 5 3 1 2 4 6 8

A catalogue record for this book is available from the British Library.

ISBN (PB): 9781788545518
ISBN (E): 9781788545495

Printed and bound by CPI Group (UK) Ltd, Croydon, CR0 4YY

GLOSSARY OF DIALECT TERMS

af – as fuck, as in 'angry af'

cba – couldn't be arsed

cya – see ya

ffs – for fuck's sake

idk – I don't know (sometimes a form of punctuation)

ikr – I know right (usually an expression of resignation or disbelief)

like – a form of verbal punctuation

lol – laughing out loud (sometimes spoken)

milf – mother I'd like to fuck

omg – oh my god

oml – oh my lord

tbf – to be fair

tbh – to be honest

Someone will kill my mother. It could be me. There is something wrong with me I know, but I see my dad thinking about it too. Only my brother loves her and she loves him idk it must be a mother-son thing like you see. She thinks she is so hot. She comes home from work full of testosterone or whatever, and if someone didn't already cook the dinner, do the washing, hoover everything including the underside of the cushions Where Dust Collects and take The Dog for a walk, it's the end of the world and there will be Shouting and Insults and People Will End Up Crying, usually me. She works for a computer company, you can't even get into her office without a retina scan, it terrifies me so I never go in. What if they can read something in your eyes? You can tell a lot from a person's eyes, like the secrets of their heart, or so I believe. Eyes can lie too, everybody knows that, but not mine. I don't think I have the brains to hide anything from anybody, I always get caught. And I have secrets. I feel like getting a retina scanner for my bedroom. Access denied, Mam. I've asked them to give me a flat. Like they have so many flats and houses. They're always evicting someone. My dad does evictions like Terminator

1

Three For Tenants In Arrears. He is a Property Addict. He can't stop buying houses because the Housing Market Crashed and Everything Is SO Cheap. It's like a hobby, it's disgusting, and we keep reading about people who don't have homes to go to. We even debated The Housing Crisis in Religion class. My Mam Never Tires Of Telling Me our religion teacher is a commie, which is ironic when you come to think of it, and she says nobody would have houses if it wasn't for people like Dad. And I think maybe my dad is causing it. Like single-handedly causing the shortage because he owns like everything almost. My dad says nothing, he just goes to the solicitors and comes home with another three-bed semi in a desirable area. He has the property gene bad. I heard someone on the radio talking about it. It goes back to the Great Famine apparently, but I don't know why my dad got it because he was never hungry a day in his life.

You just have to look at him to know that.

Like my dad has baby bellies where he should have love handles.

My mam says I'm useless and I know she's right but in school I get A1 in everything, I hardly even need to look at a book, I remember everything, absolutely everything I read. My English teacher says I remind him of a story by some South American writer, I can't pronounce the name never mind spell it, about someone who was able to remember every single thing he ever saw or heard or smelled idk I'm not that bad. Ask me to recite *Macbeth* which we are studying and I can do all the voices up to

2

Act Three where we stopped before Christmas, I can do poetry until it's Coming Out My Ears, poetry is easy. My mam says poetry is useless which is another reason I might kill her. She's only the boss's PA but she acts like she runs Computing Solutions herself. I don't even know what they make in there, some kind of software, maybe a game for mobiles, or parts of a game idk like what's so great about that? There must be a billion software companies in the world, most of them probably have retina scanners too. I couldn't care less. I'm For History and I'm For Poetry. I'm Against Technology.

She comes home with a takeaway from KFC.

I don't eat that shit.

I said I would cook some boil-in-the-bag rice and do a stir fry with whatever was in the fridge but she said no cooking two dinners, I should eat what's put in front of me. So like I didn't eat.

So now I'm anorexic.

You're going to die, she goes, you're going to die in a horrible awful way, anorexia is a terrible way to go. You'll turn into a stick and every bone in your body will hurt.

This went on all through dinner. I ate four chips. They disgust me. They are not even potato but some potato simulacrum, like a virtual potato, a Playstation Potato. When you eat it you don't feel like you've eaten except for the salt.

My dad said that Ballyshane was for sale. They were selling the house with a couple of acres and the

3

farm separately. That took the heat off me. My dad has wanted to buy Ballyshane House as long as I can remember. He even got me to do a project on it for History once. He said: The local company of the Irish Volunteers was formed up there, Captain Corry was head and tail of it, and the Black and Tans raided it so often, I remember my own father telling me about the Crossley tenders going up full of men with rifles and Glengarry caps. Right, Dad. Dad and History don't go together. I am staring at him with my mouth open. But I should have known. He knows the history of houses all right.

Holly and me say politics is just coloured stickers now. We don't have big causes to fight for like The Freedom Of Ireland or Revenge For Skibbereen. We have a Blue Party, a Green Party and a Pink Party. My dad is Blue Party. Instead of elections people should just be asked what's their favourite colour. And they should wear coloured shirts or tracksuits or something. And my dad is in well with the Blues and the Greens because of property. Blues and Greens are For Property, Pink is For The Working Man except it turns out they're For Property too lol just not saying. Like the motto for this country should be The Builders Will Save Us. I don't know what the actual motto is if we have one idk.

So I did a project on it. Old Captain Corry was dead of course, but his daughter let me look at his diaries and stuff. It wasn't proper research but it was the closest I ever came to it and I made up my mind that if my family

4

didn't eat me some fine morning because there was no porridge I would do History and become a Researcher. I would spend my life reading dead people's diaries and writing books about them. That was me. I would find forgotten people and remember them.

Are you going to buy it?

He looked at me. I'm thinking about it.

If you buy it can you buy all the furniture and stuff?

My mother rolled her eyes.

My dad said, Maybe we could. Some of it is good. There'll be an auction probably.

I don't want any of that old stuff, my mother said.

Could you buy the diaries and papers?

My dad shrugged, I have an idea the old bitch gave all that stuff to the university. Or sold it more likely.

But if she didn't?

Well, I'll be dealing with an auctioneer.

Why can't you phone her up and ask her if she'd sell it to you?

She's in America with her niece.

Well she still has to be on a mobile or something.

My dad doesn't like refusing me things. He sides with my mam about food and clothes, but if I'm asking for something he usually gives in. That's why I have a MacBook Air and an iPhone. He got me a horse for a while but I totally hate horse riding, it's not like they say in the books. I never had such a sore arse in my life and believe me I've had sore arses. Like the time I came down a slide in my short shorts and they rode up and

I got a friction burn like Third Degree. I basically fried my arse off.

I'll try, he said.

I gave him one of my looks and he winked at me.

My mother rolled her eyes again. My brother got up and tipped his bones and a few stale chips into the bin and said he was going out. My mother said not to be too late. He has a girlfriend and the whole family approves of her. She's bottle-blonde and her father has the agency for Audi. I think she's a bitch and I'm pretty sure she's two-timing my brother. I've been stalking her online. I made up a person for Facebook and got her to friend me and I'm keeping a close eye on her goings-on. She has a Twitter account too but it's mostly about make-up and I couldn't be arsed. Twitter is stupid anyway. All my friends fight because they say things on Twitter that they regret. It's the same with celebrities. First there's this OK guy who is in a band or something and he has ten million followers and then he tweets something, racism or something, and suddenly he's not in the band any more and he has like two followers and one of them is his mother. I never say anything on Twitter. Or Facebook either really. Once upon a time one of my friends tweeted about her period and she nearly committed suicide because of what people said. It's a minefield. My English teacher told us the best thing: Don't say anything on Twitter or Facebook that you wouldn't say to someone's face if your mother and father were standing beside you. That pretty much rules everything out. Like Twitter is OK for politicians saying they're cutting jobs or something, but everybody else should just shut up.

Like our local man Micky Molloy had a Twitter account and all his tweets began with the words, Great to meet with … Like, Great to meet with the reps of Farming industry this morning … or Great to meet with the Swedish ambassador yesterday … He got nicknamed Great-To-Meet Micky. It was an improvement on his previous which was Dirty Micky. Micky is Blue Party of course. His grandfather went to Spain to fight for the wrong crowd, I forget which one, we're doing the Spanish Civil War next I think, the side that won anyway. But he never fired a shot and the whole Blue Party gang got sent home because they were useless wankers. That kind of thing runs in families like wooden legs, as my grandad used to say. My grandad was Green Party in the days when only poor people were Green. If they ever were idk you couldn't always believe what my grandad said, he was a great talker. And there's another Blue Party guy called Consider It Done John Waldron. He's in a different constituency or county idk which is like a different galaxy really, we hate them because hurling. According to my dad when he says Consider It Done it's the Kiss Of Death idk why.

As soon as my brother was gone my dad said, If we sell Clarinda Park and use the flats in Paradise Street as collateral we could come up with the money. It'll be close to two mill.

I couldn't believe it. I'm like: You promised Clarinda Park for when Tony got married.

My dad gave me the silent look.

My mother said, Eat your chicken, look at you, if you don't eat you'll die.

My dad said, I'll tell you this for nothing, Suzy, it is a once in a lifetime chance. Ballyshane won't come up for sale again any time soon.

But Clarinda Park is practically their house.

But it's not. It's part of our portfolio of properties and all property is an asset to be used wisely. And I never promised it I just mentioned it once. I'd say he doesn't even remember.

Like, Dad, that so sounds crap.

Out! my mother said. Up to your room. Go. Now.

Perfect, I said, I won't have to smell that KFC shit any more.

Sometimes I can see my mother is going to hit me but she stops herself. Like there's a little tick of bones and muscles and a change in the way her hands and her body are tilted. She did that now. It always makes me flinch. To cover I got up fast.

Not a word of this to Tony, my dad said, we'll tell him when the time is right.

None of my business, I said.

Don't let us down, my dad said.

I made sure to slam the door behind me. I heard my dad calling me back to close it politely, but I ignored him. Like my dad is the King Of Letting Down. I went out for a walk. I like walking. It was a cold night with a full moon and a billion stars. They were like little bits of glass pressed against grey-blue velvet. It was so beautiful. I could hear dogs barking somewhere.

So my dad on the phone to Dan Kelleher the auctioneer. First comes Wheedling Dad: Come on now, Dan, you and me go back a long way, we soldiered together bad times and good, seriously, come on now, Dan. How many sweet deals did I set you up for? You know me and I know you. This is letting yourself down. Your father wouldn't have let me down like this. What came over you to sell so quick? You closed the sale without coming back to me. You know me, of course I'd have come up on my first offer. No way Miss Corry would have preferred selling to a Brit.

I forget which day it was but it was definitely the daytime because the one o'clock news was on and they were talking about some guy who is meant to have murdered a girl who was suicidal. Like he could have murdered half my friends. Idk we all think about it.

Then comes Angry Dad. He could do with anger management classes if they have them for property speculators. My dad is more than a tad overweight to say the least and when he gets angry it's like a machine was turned on that wasn't nailed down properly. When he comes home early from the office it's Bad News. He can fix most things. Once he said to me: There's very few problems that won't run away if you throw money at them. He has reserves or assets. Whatever.

For fuck's sake, Dan, you could have fucking rang me, Jesus. That was a serious bid. You owe me one, Dan, you owe me a fucking big one. Are you going to let this English bastard get his foot in the door? You disregarded bids before when it suited you. Are you fucking serious? You fucking bastard. By Jesus you'll be sorry. I'll fucking bury you.

Then Deadly Serious Dad: I'll tell you something for nothing, Dan Kelleher. Write this down now because I want you to remember it. This is a small town. And you can fucking forget about the party nomination. We wouldn't fucking nominate you for a run to the jakes.

He means it too. What's not generally known about my dad is that he carries grudges All The Way To The Bank And Back. One of these days he'll do something and when he does it will mean Money and probably Politics. Politics for Dad is just capitalism by other means.

He took his jacket off in his study and threw it on the floor. He was seriously pissed about Dan Kelleher. When he came out his face was the colour of Heinz Ketchup. Which is crap. I hate it. My mam puts it on everything more or less.

Make me a cup of tea, Suzy. I'm parched.

Did you hear about the real estate agent who sold a two-story house, Dad? The first story was fake and the second story didn't hold up.

He looked at me. I had the kettle in my hand. It's not an electric kettle. It's one that goes on the hob. Like I want my family to get an electric kettle like everybody else in Ireland but they say they are wasteful of money. Some electrician guy told them. My life, I swear.

That's cat, Suzy. Your jokes are really cat. Only you're so good at school, I'd march you straight in there this very minute.

Cat = crap in Dad Language.

Some English fucker blew me out of the water.

What did you bid?

One point seven. That was just an opener and that fucker Kelleher knew it too.

What did the English guy bid?

He won't say. But he says starting at one point seven it would take me ten years to get up as far as the English guy and Miss Corry wants a quick sale. He consulted with her and she just said take it. What kind of a way to sell a house is that?

What do you think he bid?

By the sound of it he was easily over two mill. Maybe two point two.

He'll probably turn out to be a relation of the Kellehers.

I could see my dad thinking about that.

They have relations in Birmingham all right. But I'd say they're not up to it.

The kettle boiled. It has a whistle thingy up its arse. Or down its throat, whichever way round it is. I made him a pot of tea. We still had Christmas cake. He likes the cake and I like the icing. He was doing something on his phone all the time, taptapping, swiping, taptapping. He looked like a blackbird, the way they stab things. A blackbird is a violent bird never mind his song. His song is beautiful.

Dad, I said, Dad.

He shook his head.

It's just gone, he said. Some fucker bought it out from under me. I can't believe it. They have sold on it on their site.

Dad, drink your tea.

He looked up at me. Squinting a little. How come I never noticed that his eyes were slightly off, the left one not exactly in line with the right?

Kelleher is putting the Castlemartin package together. I saw what he's at. It'll be big. Three, four hundred units, executive-style houses, a block of apartments, more maybe. Over my dead body. Over. My. Dead. Body, Suzy.

Dad, just let it go.

He finished his tea in one gulp. It must have burned his throat. He looked a bit stunned for a few seconds then he got a glass of water and drank it all. He stood in front of the window. It was raining. One of those sharp winter showers like someone throwing gravel at glass. Pins and needles for houses. He was going grey at the back and around the edges. Thinning too, a light circle in the middle of his head right at the top. Like a monk. Well, a monk starting out before he got the whole thing shaved. If that's what they do. Or do they just wear hats? Maybe hats make you bald, or else bald men wear hats. Old bald men do.

Ah Jesus, he said.

That was all. I was worried about him. He looked grey now. It was like the tea was way too hot. Like his throat was blistered and he couldn't talk any more. Like there was a fire in his chest burning him from the inside out.

And he went out without saying goodbye. I heard him driving off.

Then my mam came home. It's like one of those silent movies where they go in one door and out another. The Three Stooges whatever. Except just two.

Where is Dad?

He went out.

He texted me to say he was here.

He was but he went out again. The house is gone.

I know. I can't believe it, it only went on the market on Monday, the Kellehers are behind this, mark my words.

I pointed at the teapot. It's fresh enough, want me to pour you a cup?

Why are you home today? There's nothing wrong with you.

Tea and cake, I said.

I'll tea-and-cake you if you don't go to school tomorrow, Miss.

I will, Mam.

She stared at me. Sometimes I think she's wondering who I am. She was wearing her Max Mara suit. I have to admit my mam can look pretty cool. My friend Holly said she was a milf. I seriously wonder about Holly sometimes. She could be bi or lesbian. But she liked Ed Sheeran. I have nothing against gays. In fact we used to have a gay friend, a boy who was in our Primary. He turned out to be gay by about fourteen, but Holly and me always knew. He had four sisters. Anyway, the three of us palled around a lot, but in the end his family moved away. They went to Australia because the dad lost his job.

Once, in Primary, Miss Daly said, Holly, what's your full name? Holly said, Holly. The teacher said: But what's it short for? It's not short for anything, Miss. Holly, what is your full Christian name? I'm not a Christian, Miss, my parents are hippies.

It was true too. Her parents lived in a cottage with an acre and they raised all their own food, vegetarian of course, although Holly eats meat when she's not at home, and totally organic. Everybody called them The Hippies. I used to let Holly copy my homework and I'd show her where to put in mistakes. Once she found a robin with a broken leg, she picked him up with both hands and carried him home. I would not touch a bird, ew, I swear, the idea of touching something with feathers. I would die before I would do that. Holly tells jokes. I don't know where she hears them. Maybe she makes them up. What do Waterford people call Viagra? Willy Power. I don't get it. She tells me that William Power is a common name in Waterford. I still don't get it. I googled it and William is not actually all that common. Power is a Waterford name all right.

15

The cottage looks down on Inch beach and I know my dad or Kelleher the auctioneer would give their right hands to have the selling of it. It is a desirable residence in spades – not the house, the first thing a developer would do would be to level it. They'd level it with Holly and The Hippies inside if they thought they could get away with it. They tend to see the law as an Unfortunate Accident that prevents wealth creation. Like, ever hear a developer defending a forest or a green field?

Go on so, make a fresh cup, my mam said. And before the tea was even drawn Dad texted from the car to say that it was two point five mill and that he wouldn't have been able to go there. My mam read me the text, which was like an achievement because he never uses punctuation. 2.5 mill some English celeb I couldn't go that high he blew me off so much for buy Irish you would think Kelleher would have some f***ing loyalty so much for support your own. Like in texts my Dad won't say fucking. Like it'll be all ★★★. But he'll say it in words all right.

Your dad is very upset about Ballyshane, she said.

I said I knew.

I hate when he gets like this.

I knew that too.

I'm worried about what he'll do.

I shrugged. I know I shouldn't shrug, I've been warned, but sometimes a shrug is all there is. What can you say? My dad will do whatever he wants. You can't talk to him. My mam is the last person that could say anything. She has like two registers, as my English teacher would say, normal and ballistic. Usually I can shrug invisibly. It's like my shrugs take place in a parallel universe or a different reality, nobody notices, I shrug and everything is the same before and after. But today she saw me. She pointed her finger at me.

Don't you shrug at me, Suzy Regan. If your father has a heart attack I know who to blame.

I burst into tears. I legit hate tears. My mam took one look at me and made that face that says, How did I give birth to something like you?

Just do what you're told and go to school tomorrow. He has enough stress.

She got up and walked out. I heard her peeing then flushing in the downstairs toilet, sound-proofing in my house is shit Even Though We Have Gold Taps, then running water, the front door slamming. Then she was gone. Outside it was a February day which is meant to be the start of spring and idk but things did look a bit crisper, like there was life starting deep down. But it was a cold blue day and the sky was hard as ice. It looked like it might shatter and fall in. It would lacerate the world and all who sailed in it. The broken glass of the universe falling on our hearts like love.

So, OK, this is not going to be a confession. But you know, I was seventeen and I dreamed of what it would be like to have a man inside me. I tried some things, you can imagine, or you'll have to imagine, because this is not turning into anything like that. So get over it. And it's not going to be like History either, no jigsaw puzzle pieces falling into place. Maybe sometime in the future, like after the Leaving or something, I'll be able to look back and say, Now I understand it. But I doubt it. Because we are not Living Through History, like Miss Leahy the Religion teacher says. Instead we are Living Through Random Shit, which is what Miss Regan, aka Me, says.

But what I'm trying to say is I was ready for something to happen and it did. But picture my surprise when it turned out not to be about sex. Like when you're in the teenage-girl demographic you think the only thing that can happen is like losing your virginity to a Harry Styles lookalike. I legit wanted to lose it to Harry Styles from One Direction when I was fourteen. I would have settled for losing it to a fan even.

But the first thing that happened was that my dad's heart was broken. It must have been breaking for a long time, or holding together too hard. Just because it wasn't what I was imagining, but some kind of like total car crash in which people died not me, doesn't mean it wasn't something. I tell myself: Never forget this. What happens every step of the way.

But I will forget it. As you do.

So idk why property is such a big thing for my dad. Like who would endure heartbreak for a fucking desirable res on circa whatever acres? But you have to think it is a Georgian house with a fanlight over the door. And those windows you can walk through. Old Miss Corry told me: The Corrys have been here for two hundred years. She said it like she was standing up for herself, like I was the enemy. This was at the time when I did the project for Local History. The Corrys were the project so like I Get It. But then I'm not The British. The British were the only enemy Ireland ever had. How could I be the enemy ffs. Anyway We The Regans have been here for two hundred years too But We Never Had A Fanlight. My dad's ambition was to put that fanlight in the family.

So the English guy moved in.

I expected there would be architects and renovations, new central heating, solar panels, works on the grounds. That's what celebs do, right?

But the old guy just moved in and expelled the rats. He had a housekeeper that he brought with him from England. She bought food in the local supermarket a few times and then she discovered Aldi. People said she had a real *Eastenders* accent, but I don't think there's an *Eastenders* accent. And if there was nobody around here would know it. It's just anything English that doesn't sound like Shakespeare or the Queen. The Queen of England To Be Precise, as Holly says. I knew someone was in Ballyshane before anybody because I saw the smoke from the heating boiler. There was a lot of smoke. I said to Holly, They need to get that boiler serviced. We could see the smoke from the school bus.

It might blow up, she said.

I could see she would like an explosion.

Of course Holly doesn't do science. I told her diesel boilers don't explode. As far as I know. Idk I'm not sure. But then she prefers the idea of the explosion. Holly has a strong sense of justice. She would have been throwing bombs at kings once upon a time, but she def would not throw herself under a horse. When she gets mad she gets a red line above her left eye. That is a mark from where she was hit by a see-saw when she was a child. Someone jumped off just as she was jumping on. She had stitches and concussion. She always says she doesn't remember whether she had concussion or not because she had concussion. Which is true when you think about it. Like it's just hearsay, the concussion.

That evening I walked The Dog up to Ballyshane. I like the bare trees. Winter still, never mind the calendar. They are as pale as bones in the moonlight. The dark is not scary.

All the lights were on. Miss Corry always closed the curtains, she liked her privacy, I suppose you get used to it when your residence is set in circa two hundred acres with a tree-lined drive. But the English guy didn't give a shit. I could actually see him sitting in a room with a glass of something in his hand, watching the telly. English people drink gin and tonic. My guess is that he was just under five feet tall. I'm not tall myself but he would be six inches smaller than me at least. He was like a rasher of wind, as my grandad used to say, he was so thin. You wouldn't think someone as thin as that would be able to stand up. He was about fifty per cent bald and the bald place was really shiny.

Even outside the window I could feel the heat. My mother would kill him for keeping the place so hot. She says it's unhealthy and bad for the environment. My mam doesn't give a flying fuck about the environment as a matter of fact, but she hates people to be comfortable. My house is always cold unless my mam is cold and then it's too hot. My dad just says wear a sweater. Like sometimes I wear two. And I have been known to wear a woolly cap in bed. My life I swear.

I took a pic from fairly far back with the flash turned off. It was OK. I WhatsApped it to Holly. Guess where I am?!!?

She replied: OMG dont get caught.

It was cold and The Dog already peed on every bush and brick on circa two hundred acres/circa eighty hectares and it was time to go, and I wanted to go because, although I am a natural-born snoop, it gets a bit boring after a while unless people do things. A murder would

23

be nice. But something made me stay a bit longer and sure enough something interesting happened. The door opened. The housekeeper came in. She was a lot taller than the English guy, taller than me too, maybe six feet. She had big bones and big hands and a flat ass. She wore skinny jeans, a skin-tight silky T-shirt and high boots and I just knew she was a man. Even though she could wear those high boots like a model, even though she moved like a model, even though she did not do a single thing that was like gay or something, I knew she was a man. She had that perfect English complexion. In that instant I fell in love with her skin. I wanted it. I would wear it like a suit of designer clothes. In the lamplight I could see that it was flawless.

She went and sat on another chair. They spoke to each other for a second, then turned their eyes on the telly. There was nothing to say they were in love but I knew they were. They sat there like an old couple watching the six o'clock news.

I did not tell Holly.

It's not that I don't tell Holly everything, it's just I don't think she's ready for things sometimes.

And tbf nothing much happens in our lives, Holly and me, just a lot of talk. Boys have sports. All the boys we know play hurling and football. I don't know if they talk about us but we talk about them a lot. And when we're not talking we're texting or WhatsApp. It's not that we fancy them. It's just they're there, and they're something else, and they don't go to my school which is all girls so we hardly ever actually talk to them. But one thing did happen to Holly. Going home from school once she was attacked by two boys. They tried to pull her into a field. She didn't go. But she said they tried to get their hands up her skirt and stuff. Like you see. Lucky for her a car came along and she legged it. Holly is fast. She does athletics. They could have caught her too but they were afraid they would be seen from the car. This happened when she was nearly fourteen. She was an early developer. She was the first girl in our class to start to show on top. And now she's a bit big. She says she'll get breast reduction when she's working. Anyway, she says she thought they were bottlers and nothing would have happened but idk. That's how it happens.

We were in Tesco's café and we saw Jason and Helen, who are a couple, passing a cigarette around mouth to mouth. Maybe the café does not belong to Tesco idk but it's next door. They didn't even kiss or hold hands. They just stood in the cold and smoked. And when it was finished they stubbed it out in a flower pot and went indoors again. Is that supposed to be love? If so it is not for me or Holly. Holly said she would never marry because marriage is a bourgeois institution. Well, I said, I'm pretty bourgeois and I'm not going to marry either.

Holly had a turkey BLT followed by strawberry flan and I had an apple turnover. Holly asked me if I fancied Jason and I said no way. And I hate smoking. What if it was some celebrity who smoked? Some actor? Or Niall Horan? Or… I stopped her right there. Do not mention Niall Horan in my presence, and smoking is an absolute no-no, it is so just ew. She giggled. Her dad smoked marijuana or hash, I'm not sure which and she said she liked the smell of it. He never smoked it when I was around but the smell sort of lingered a bit. It was nice actually. I'm not against soft drugs. Holly gave me all the cream from her strawberry flan and I gave her the walnuts from my apple turnover. She just wanted the flan part. We had one pot of tea between us. The girl gave me a look when I asked for two cups.

Holly is lactose intolerant. It gives her Flatulence and Bloating. She is embarrassed by it. Her tummy sounds like a gunfight in an empty barrel. But since she gave up lactose she was totally normal.

But the truth is we both envied Jason and Helen. Or at least we envied Helen. Neither of us had ever been kissed except by each other, which doesn't count, it doesn't even feel right because we both know boys are rough, especially if they haven't shaved recently. Helen is a bitch. Like the minute Jason asked her out she tweeted it. It was like she won the lottery, the way people who win the lottery sometimes stop talking to their friends and family in case people ask them for money. And the first time they kissed – tweeted. He made her stop. She told Mary Doyle that he said he didn't want his game all over Twitter. We all thought game was a shit thing to say. But she told Mary Doyle the first time they had sex and Mary Doyle told everyone even though she didn't tweet it. And she also said they didn't use protection and now everyone is wondering how long it will take Helen to get pregnant. And I think all of that is just so crap. It makes me sad af.

So my fake Facebook identity. I discovered that on my brother's girlfriend's timeline there was hate stuff about my brother. My brother is on Twitter but he's not on Facebook. Well he was, but he got bullied so he came off it. The hate stuff was not from her, but from her friends. They were bitching about him. Like he's always well turned out. He likes clothes. He dresses well. He's not exactly metro, but he's getting there. So this girl is like, He's so faggy, he makes me sick. And another time, Why u going out with that faggot? And another time, Does he take pipe? Like I don't even know what take pipe means but I think I do. I wrote back on the wall: Bitches you should mind your own business stuff ur hate messages up ur arses. I got unfriended so fast. And blocked. And that was the end of the surveillance of my brother's girlfriend. But I found out about the girl who was doing the hate message stuff. She was some kind of a third cousin of my friend Serena. I've met some of Serena's family and every single one of them is a religious creeper. Like once Serena and me turned up at a cousins's house at tea-time and they were all kneeling down saying the rosary except for the grandmother or maybe the great-grandmother idk and it was just so weird. Like seriously creepy. I don't know about this girl, but Serena told me she was a bitch. She was doing Dental. Serena said she should have been doing Mental. It's hard to know if you can trust Serena on anything. But for a long time I was plotting some kind of retribution except I didn't know what. Nobody does that to my brother.

My brother is in Uni doing Elec Eng. Elec is short for electronic not electric. His mates Tosser Kennedy and John Brown are doing Civil. They make some kind of a team, probably the losing team. A team of hopeless cases. Going by their stories they spend most their time in Keniry's pub worrying about where they can get the notes for the last lecture or whether the lecturer cba to put them online. I'm not looking forward to the day my dad finds out he's doing Elec. My dad thinks he's doing Real Eng, like he'll be building houses that my dad will own.

My dad doesn't talk to my brother. For example, he can't stand to be in the same room as him except to eat. This is like the most dangerous thing in the world to me. Like building your house on a volcano idk. It's going to be terrible.

But my brother goes out every morning just after me and he gets home usually late. And I don't know what he does all day because he doesn't seem to go to lectures.

My mam loves my brother because he was the first.

Or because he is a boy idk.

She never even looks at me unless she has to. I'm invisible.

Or I'm not invisible enough.

One day Holly and me were walking on Inch strand. The tide was low and the sand was like a war zone, seaweed everywhere. There were birds idk maybe oystercatchers even though there's no oysters that anybody ever noticed. And there was no one else there. And I said to Holly, I'm so unhappy, Holly.

I never said that to anyone before. But Holly understood. She caught my hand and we just walked around the strand like that, holding hands, and it was like the most perfect moment of my life ever.

My brother. Sometimes I think I love him more than anyone and sometimes I hate him. Like when I was sick once he sat with me all night. When I woke up in the morning he was there asleep in a chair. And another time he told me how lonely he was. Aw. And then there was the time that I told him I was depressed and he came out of his bedroom and handed me a pack of razor blades. It took me a while to work out what they were for. I looked it up on the net. Some of those blogs are terrible. They made me sad. Then another time when we were at the beach he took our dog out into the water and held him by the tail so he couldn't swim for shore. Then he started to push him down. I didn't realise what was happening. He was laughing. When I saw what he was doing I told my mam and she just laughed. My brother can do anything and she never says a word to him. I said, He'll die, Mam, The Dog is going to drown. Don't be stupid, she said, it's his dog, he's not going to hurt him. And there's another thing. When he got The Dog everybody had an idea what to call him but my brother said, His name is The Dog. Then the time he discovered superglue. He tried to superglue a butterfly's wing to the bulb of his reading light but the superglue burned through the wing so you had a butterfly with a hole in its wing trying to fly. And another time he superglued the locks in one of his teacher's cars. Like the teacher was a wanker but that must have cost him a fortune. My brother thought it was completely funny. And then another time there was snow and my bus didn't turn up and I was on my own at the bus stop and it was getting dark and he walked three miles through the snow with a warm coat and a pair of boots and waited with me until my mam got out of work. I would have frozen to death and got frostbite but for him. He got his driving licence at eighteen on the first attempt and after that he often came to pick me up from school on really bad days. But I put a stop to it because of this one time. He was like doing a hundred in a sixty zone. When I asked him to slow down he started to swing the wheel. Every time we passed another car he swung the wheel towards it and straightened out at the last second. People were blowing horns. Like he could have killed us and half a dozen other people. I'm surprised nobody sent for the guards, but maybe people recognised my mam's car. It's an Audi A5 Sportback. While we're dodging killing people, he decided to tell a joke. Like the joke is: This German car salesman gets his wife to have sex with four springs under her and blowing on a duck caller, and when she asks him why, he says he was at a sales conference and they were all talking about this brilliant four-sprung-duck technique.

I figured it must be an engineering thing.

But by the end of it we were up to a hundred and twenty coming into a bad bend. We got around it all right. I felt the blood going cold in my face. I nearly fainted. I was convinced he was trying to commit suicide.

Then another time my mam sent him to pick me up from Holly's house one night and he had a bottle of vodka and he wanted me to drink. I said no, vodka is ew. So he started swigging it instead. Like driving me home at midnight on a wet night. When we got home I said, Tony, I will never get into a car with you again and if Mam sends you tell her I won't go with you, because if you come and collect me I'll fucking walk home, get it? I slammed the door. The light came on in my parents' bedroom and when I was going upstairs my dad came out. What's up, Suzy? Did I hear you two fighting? Just ask Tony, I said. But he didn't. He went back to bed. My father never does anything like that. If something needs to be faced, Mam faces it, but she will be ballistic before she even starts, so Dad doesn't tell her stuff.

So it was Tony who first spoke to the English guy and found out his name was Tom Bowles.

He was meant to be a writer but I googled him and there is no writer called Tom Bowles. At least there is a newspaper reporter from America who got fired for clapping at Daytona. I don't know what Daytona is. I know I could google it, but seriously, life is too short. Then there is someone called Tom Parker Bowles who is a relative of the Queen of England and came

33

out in support of gay marriage. Bollocks to the anti-gay marriage rabble, he said. I didn't know that's how you spelled bollocks, it's not in the *Fallons Spelling Book*. Anyway, as Holly said, you can be in favour of gay marriage and still be a useless parasite, *c'est la vie*, baby. Sometimes Holly says, *C'est la vie*, baby, and I always think it's something from a film but not one I've ever seen. So if this Tom Bowles was a writer and he was rich enough to buy Ballyshane for like Monopoly Money, what did he write? Google knows everything. Of course he might just be a crap writer that even Google never heard of but who won the EuroMillions lottery. My brother met him in some pub in town, he said. But I say that is crap because whatever pub my brother goes to, a rich English writer named Tom Bowles is not going to be there.

I said, Describe him.

He said, Small and thin, like tiny almost a midget. He's completely fucking ancient. I would say he's eighty.

What did he say to you?

He said, Can you get a drink here? The place was jointed. He just didn't think he'd make it to the bar at his height.

And you said?

I said you could. I said I'd get one for him like the bar was six deep and he goes, Thank you so much, in a real English accent, you know what I mean, like totally Hugh Grant.

Not *Eastenders*?

So not *Eastenders*.

I was pretty sure he was telling the truth but I can never really tell. People lie to me all the time. My friend Serena who I now get hate messages from once told me we were sisters forever. Then she went somewhere on her holidays, Fuerteventura I think, and she sent me selfies for a week, one every day at some beach or in a restaurant, and when she came back she hated me. That was over a year ago. We never go on holidays except to West Kerry Cottages for a week although once they told me we were going To Go To Rome But We Never. I even watched *Gladiator* on Netflix even though it's total bullshit and I saw it before, that's how much I believed in it.

Once my brother's phone ass-called me. I could hear club music in the background. Idk what kind of a club. I have never been inside one. My mam won't let me. Neither has Holly. We are probably the last girls in our class to do it. I just hope it's worth waiting for.

I often get ass-calls from him. Another time I could hear shooting. I guessed it was a computer game but it sounded real. And another time there was no talking but I knew he was drunk. I don't know how I knew that. It was about four in the afternoon. The strange thing about families are there are too many things you can't say. You would think that you could say anything to your family, but you can't. And sometimes people tell you something and it's Too Much Information. Like sometimes you don't need to know. So I suppose that means that I don't want people to tell me things either.

So I'm like halfway between withholding information and calling a press conference.

And why do I know he's ass-calling me? Maybe he calls and doesn't want to say anything, maybe he just wants to hear a human voice. Or maybe he can't say.

My brother had a friend called John Brown who was actually brown. His grandfather was French and he married an Algerian woman. Like his father came from Algeria. He was an aircraft engineer, but he died in a tragic and ironic accident with a Flymo lawnmower. He got electrocuted. Some people call John Nigger Brown but I hate that kind of racist shit. John Brown is so sweet. Whenever he comes to see my brother he Talks To Me For Five Minutes. When I was thirteen I was in love with John Brown but then he got a girlfriend and I decided that I couldn't be in love with him because it would be like home-breaking. Not many big boys will talk to a girl for five minutes. He would come into my house and see me sitting at the kitchen table doing my homework and he'd come over and sit beside me.

What are you working on?

Sums.

This was in Primary when we said Sums instead of Maths. I would be like doing long division or something. Our teacher hated calculators. She said, You can't use a calculator when you're buying three ice-creams and three cokes and you'll never know if you got the right

37

change. Yeah, well, I can add in my head and you don't need long division to work out the cost of three ice-creams and three cokes. But anyway, she had a point. Just, most of the people in my class used calculators at home anyway, their parents didn't care. Holly used one. She was useless where calculations were concerned, although she was pretty good at estimating, which we were supposed to do too but I couldn't be arsed. I'd just put down the right answer and then write down a wrong answer that was close enough.

He goes, Oh, long division. Serious stuff.

Like he went to college to do Engineering. And even then he was top of his class for Maths. He used to do my brother's homework. So I knew he was just being nice to me, and when people are nice to me I nearly always cry. Like I cry at the IKEA ad, the one where all the clothes fly through the little boy's bedroom window and land all folded in the IKEA storage modules? As soon as I see the little boy standing at the window looking out I cry. So then it was, What's wrong? Is everything OK?

Sometimes he'd give me a big hug. Aw.

So he did well in school. He got Engineering. He came second in his class. He got a girlfriend – a new one in college. I met her. I knew as soon as I saw her that she was crazy about him. She was a keeper. They were like night and day. He was tall and well-built and as brown as some kind of really nice old wood. She was tiny, blonde, small in every way, as pale as snow. They were like a couple from a book, or from an old story. He was the exact opposite of my brother who couldn't be arsed to get out of bed three days a week, who never went to a lecture if he knew someone who would give him the notes or if he knew they'd be online in time. John Brown went to every lecture. Sometimes when we talked he told me about brilliant engineering projects he had studied, like bridges, or skyscrapers built on rafts so they could stand up in sand, or the Thames flood barrier. All sorts of things. The one that really got him going was the Large Hadron Collider. He told me all about it and when they started it up he was all excitement. He showed me a YouTube video about it. What Is The LHC And How Does It Work? I remember things, but not everything. The protons are accelerated to ninety-nine per cent of the speed of light. Giga electron volts. All that shit. But I didn't understand what they were talking about.

I remember once he was in our kitchen and he grabbed me and made me look at a tree and there was this huge crow perched on the outside of a branch and the branch was bending so much we thought he'd fall off, and then the crow started to shuffle sideways step by step until he got into a strong part of the branch. We were laughing our asses off.

That crow gets Euler–Bernoulli Theory, he said. Yay for plastic bending!

Engineers! Like the branch wasn't even plastic. And who the fuck are Oiler and Bernoulli? But my brother never talked about this stuff. I know programming languages and microchips are not exactly hot, but yeah.

I saw one of his textbooks once. *Introduction to Digital Systems: Modelling, Synthesis, and Simulation Using VHDL.* Now that's definitely catchier than *Pride and Prejudice.* And it cost a hundred and thirty-five euro. It was a laugh a minute: the present states are the outputs of flip-flops. Therefore to use J-K flip-flops to implement sequential circuits, inputs J and K must be determined from the output states of the J-K flip-flop. So that's OK. Next time I go to the pool I'll remember to bring J and K.

I hate the way my brother's friends talk to each other. They call each other things. Cunt. Knobhead. Dick. Wanker. Knob-jockey. Gay. They don't even think about what it means. Like sometimes I think it's their way of saying they love each other. If boys love each other idk. Maybe. History does not record.

One time him and my brother took me on a trip to see a new bridge somewhere. It was perf. I got to sit where I could look at John's neck. He had like a totally flawless neck. It was a pale brown colour and had no lines. The hair was trimmed exactly right and it was as black as coal and tightly curled. He never shaved it. He wasn't the shaved-head kind of guy. My brother's neck was the exact opposite. It was grey because he never washed it only rinsed himself in the shower. It had pimples, like totally gross pimples. His hair was always sticking up. The necks of his collars always had Blood Spots, oml. I never wanted to look at my brother's neck. John Brown was excited because this was the bridge with the Longest Single Span in Ireland, like totally a Cable-Stayed

Bridge, with a tower of A Hundred And Twelve Metres! Like it was completed NEARLY A YEAR EARLY!!!! Imagine the excitement! He was practically having an engineering orgasm every five minutes in the passenger seat in front of me. It was one small step for mankind to imagine what he'd be like having a human one. I almost had one myself watching him.

We drove east for nearly two hours and it was morning and the sun was in the side window all day. And at some point I fell asleep as you do. Faintly in my sleep I heard my brother say, She's out cold. And John Brown said, She's so cute when she's asleep. I wanted to wake up and say, WHAT ABOUT WHEN I'M AWAKE FFS??!!?? And my brother said, That's about the only time she's cute. And they laughed. And I knew they were being OK about me and I just went deep. I woke up about twenty minutes later and they were talking about something else.

John Brown said, I don't know.

My brother said, Come on, Nigger, it's mad like.

I have exams in a couple of weeks.

It's always work with you for fuck's sake. Man, get a life.

Faith would kill me.

Fuck Faith. She's never going to know.

So at that point I guessed that we were approaching something that always upsets me – the Moment Of Embarrassing Revelation. And I did what I always do. I fucked up. I sat up suddenly and said, Where are we, guys?

My brother gave me a hard look in the rear-view mirror. It was maybe a bit like a retina scan.

How long are you awake?

I rubbed my eyes to make it realistic and said, I just woke up. What's up?

John Brown shook his head and looked out the window at the passing fields. My brother indicated suddenly that he was overtaking and pulled right out into the other lane. Suddenly we were passing three cars and an artic. The lorry driver blew his horn like crazy. A car coming towards us swerved onto the hard shoulder. Another car flashed lights. Eventually we were clear but we were still on the wrong side.

For fuck's sake, John Brown said, pull in, you fucking wanker.

Suddenly my brother let go of the wheel. He put his hands up. The car continued for five seconds in a straight line and then began to curve gently into the far ditch. I was like literally frozen to the seat. I could not move a muscle. Then John grabbed the wheel and guided us to our own side and my brother took over and we were OK again. I don't know. Maybe we weren't OK. It's hard to know. John Brown said, What the fuck was that about? And my brother just shrugged. Will you or won't you? he said. John Brown said, Since you ask me so nicely.

Whatever it was, it would be bad news.

Anything bad that has ever happened to John Brown happened because of my brother. So I should have stayed quiet, pretended to be asleep. Maybe if I could have known what it was I could have headed him off. Maybe. Idk.

Like I remember my brother daring John Brown to drive a motorbike in a field. He knew and I knew that John could not drive a pedal bike, never mind a motorbike. But John did it. Because John couldn't say no to my brother. Like every stupid thing he ever did was my brother's doing. So he took off across the field and he panicked and just kept getting faster. We had to take him to the hospital, me pressing with both hands on his calf where his skin was shredded. He bled all over the back seat. He never said a word only gave me a look that said, How stupid am I? Or maybe it said, Your brother is a complete dickhead. Possibly THE complete dickhead. They gave him eleven stitches and some debriding, whatever that is. They also gave him a local anaesthetic which wore off on the way home. That was not fun.

So I was at home one evening and my brother got a text. It was from a friend. He read it and went pale.

Fuck, he said.

What's wrong? my mam said.

Nigger is dead.

I burst into tears. My mother stared at him. My father said, How did it happen?

They pulled his body out of the river.

I could hear wailing and it took me a few seconds to work out that it was me. My brother was just opening and closing his mouth. Then he rushed out of the room.

Oh Jesus, my mother said, it must have been suicide.

Don't jump to conclusions, my dad said, it was a right bad night last night. He might have got blown in.

Don't be stupid, my mother said.

My dad shut up. The Dog left the room.

My mam said, He broke up with Faith, of course.

My brother left the phone on the table when he ran. I picked it up and looked at it. *U hr nigger dead fire brigade pulled body out of river a hour ago fuckin random u hear anthing?* I threw it on the floor. The back casing came off and spun away somewhere and it started to ring for some reason. It was a shite phone anyway.

Pick that up, my mother said.

I just walked. I am pro at walking out. Come back here, she shouted, come back here, come back down here this minute. But she didn't come after me. If she did I wouldn't be responsible for my deeds. I would tear her eyes out I swear. I went to my room and cried for three hours. And all that time I could hear my brother crying in the next room and sometimes hitting things. I fell asleep first.

Serena and Holly and Me. All through Primary that was the gang. Holly is a dote. She has these pale green eyes that are to die for. When she smiles they glow like that stuff inside a seashell idk some kind of pearl. Serena has long blond hair and eyes of blue and her figure is perf but her smile is the smile of a dead pollock. It just doesn't work. She talks posh too. She was in America until she was seven. Her father Is A Surgeon. I don't know for which part, maybe eyes. He used to have a head of brown hair but now he has a receding hairline and a comb-over like half a dozen shoelaces frayed at the ends. He makes a shitload on Private of course and he takes my dad's advice and buys into property. Like my dad would identify an opportunity and phone around and see if people were interested. This was at a time when he was seriously growing his portfolio and he needed investors. But then the arse fell out of everything and now he gets complaints in writing from people who put money into things. He points out that there are no guarantees and the value of property may fall as well as rise. As they say.

Serena's family are religious. They got it in America. I don't really get the religion thing tbf.

Our parish priest is a Five Star Grade A Nutter. Once I heard him give a sermon at a funeral and he compared a dead person to a chicken coming out of the oven. Like the person wasn't even being cremated. The coming out of the oven part was when the person got to heaven. I wanted to shout, But they're going to eat him! Like who would want to go to heaven if a bunch of your family and friends were waiting around at the other end with a knife and a fork? He is An Absolute Spacer.

And around that time Serena went to Fuerteventura, and that was that. It's hate messages now. U fckin slag I hate u. Nobody likes u ur useless. I usd to lik u b4 but u were betr then. U have no frens. I hate your guts sht I hate you so much. Like quoting McBusted is a lethal weapon. But I don't give a shit. I just know what she's like. If she punctuated them and spelled them right I might take more interest. I couldn't be arsed to block her.

But she did one thing I will never forgive her for. She told people I was lesbian and I was with Holly. That was the end of her for me. Like, whatever about hating me, she didn't have to do that to Holly.

Calling people lesbian was like an emerging trend in our class.

I never told Holly but she found out anyway. She told me. I said I was mortified about it. She said she didn't give a fuck, and maybe we should do it anyway since we had the name for it. The two of us fell down laughing at that. Holly is one chick who doesn't swing both ways. Her family is weird. Sometimes I think her dad really is an anarchist or a communist or whatever he says he is. My brother says he's an ageing hippy. They have books. Like in my family the only room with books is my bedroom. Holly has read more books than me.

Holly wanted me to fix Serena but I'm not getting into that shit. And she didn't have a plan anyway. So.

My dad was complaining about chest pains. My mam said it was stress because of Ballyshane and like his plan of vengeance on Dan Kelleher. Like Dad was so George Bush. And that made Dan Kelleher Saddam Hussein and look where that went. And then she said it was indigestion because he was eating too fast. Like my mam should be a qualified surgeon or something. Then she said he was getting an ulcer. Then she said he was stressing because he thought he was having a heart attack and he couldn't be because he didn't have a pain down his left arm. When he got a pain down his left arm she took him to the Lighthouse Clinic which is Private so you get an appointment immediately and they did tests and said his heart was perfect and he had indigestion and a doctor there gave him a prescription for something to fix his digestion. I googled it and it was true. It was a proton pump inhibitor and it suppressed the production of excess acid, but the things it was used for were scarier than a heart attack. So idk. I'm scared. I'm so scared.

My dad said the Lighthouse place was cat. He hated flowers and people calling him Sir. Would you take a seat, Sir? Would you fill out this form, Sir? Can you settle your account in advance please, Sir? Sir is cat to him. He says it's English. But Americans say it too. Like boys say Sir to their dads. At least on TV. It's totally bizarre. Like having a flag on a flag-pole outside your house. Like even who wants a flag pole in the garden? Even if you didn't put a flag on it? It's weird.

And then he went to a point-to-point meeting. I was meant to go but I got a cold and stayed at home. My mam was at work. And at the point-to-point meeting Dad met Dan Kelleher and they had an argument. My dad accused Kelleher of taking a finder's fee. Then he went for a drink with some friends and drove home. He went straight to bed. Then I was really scared. Like my dad never goes to bed before midnight. My mam refused to check him out. She said he needed to sleep. He was tired. He had a tiring day. I went upstairs myself but I could hear him snoring so I didn't go in. Later I heard him in the toilet. I went to my room because I could hear better from there. He came out of the toilet and went back to bed. An hour later I heard him in there again. He flushed twice. I heard him coughing. Then he went back to bed and soon I heard him snoring. By then it was eleven o'clock at night. I heard my mam coming upstairs. She usually goes to bed at eleven. It takes her half an hour to take her make-up off and everything. Their bathroom is en-suite but my dad prefers to use the main one. I heard them talking. Then it was silence. I did not fall asleep. I sat on my bed reading until after one o'clock, then I lay down reading. About three o'clock I woke to hear the toilet flushing again. I knew it was my dad. I got up and went to my door. I looked out and saw him going into the bedroom. I saw that my mam was awake. The light was on and she was sitting up. I closed the door again because, whatever was happening, it was too much. I heard them talking. I could not hear what they were saying but not being able to hear pissed me off so much. I put my earphones in and listened to Beyoncé. I like deeply hate Beyoncé but I paid for the album. I fell asleep listening to 'Pretty Hurts'.

And in the morning he was fine. He was a bit paler than yesterday. He had his breakfast. Did we keep you awake last night? Nope, I just couldn't sleep. Don't be worried. I'm not. I'm fine. I know, Dad.

He was irritable though. Turn off that radio, Suzy.

It was a report on the trial thingy. The guy who groomed the suicide ideation woman. It was so fucking weird. Like Five Hundred Shades of Grey. Five thousand even.

How can I digest my breakfast with that stuff going on? It would put you off your food.

Like nothing would put my dad off his food, even if it was irradiated by a nuclear explosion or if it was alive. My dad would eat a person if he needed to.

TURN OFF THE RADIO I HEARD ENOUGH ABOUT BONDAGE!

OK, Dad.

But I was soooo not wanting to turn it off. I would google it later.

Like I don't know what happened to him during the night because as I said, nobody in my family told me anything. I was supposed to feel safe and secure

because the house IS FULL OF FUCKING SECRETS.
Jesus wept twice. It's like we're the fucking government
except there's no WikiLeaks. Or a secret society. A Regan
NEVER TALKS.

That was the day that Serena picked to be nice to
me. She sat beside me in English. She didn't say anything
but I knew she was doing something. Like there are five
empty desks in English. Then when the bell went and
Mr Drew went out she passed me a note. I didn't see
her writing during the class which means she wrote it
Before. It was a piece from her A4 pad and it was folded
in four. I looked at her. She didn't look at me. She stared
at the blackboard.

What's this?

Just read it.

Why can't you fucking tell me, you're sitting right
here?

She looked away.

So I unfolded the letter. It said: Hi Suzy.

I swear. It was Hi Suzy, like it was after arriving in
the post. And it was signed Serena xx. At least she didn't
have her address and the date.

Hi Suzy,

*I am so sorry. I have been a bitch. I don't know what got in
to me. You are still my best friend and I am so so sorry.*

Yours sincerely,

Serena xx

I got one of my hot flushes. Why idk. I just coloured up. My face got hot and then my neck got hot and then I could feel it spreading down over my boobs. Inside my clothes I'm a neon sign that says FOR FUCK'S SAKE. I couldn't believe it. Orla Power saw it and she stared at me. Then she looked at Serena. She said, This is like fucking lesbian central. She walked before I could think of anything to say.

That was your fault, I said to Serena.

I know.

I folded the letter again. I thought about giving it back to her. Then I unfolded it and read it again. Then I folded it again. Like I could origami for Ireland.

Like why didn't you just say it? Like you're sitting here beside me for the past fifty minutes?

She says: Please?

In that voice she can do. Like Princess Serena.

I'm like: OK, but no more fucking hate messages, OK?

Cool, she goes.

The she starts to pack her books. Just like that.

I have Biology, she says, I'm late. Did you see the thing about the murder last night on the news? Talk to you later.

I don't do Biology. Not as a subject. My next class was History and Holly was in it too. We were supposed to do some writing in the middle so we got a chance to talk. I told Holly about Serena. She said she would try to find out what was going on. We were both agreed that Serena was just too much.

After big break, in Maths, she told me that everyone was saying that Serena was a bitch and nobody was her friend any more. A couple of people even unfriended her. Like unfriending is the nuclear option in my school. So now we're the three musketeers.

We were supposed to be problem-solving. Maths is all this shit now, problem-solving and approximation and guessing and several right answers and I hate it. In the old days there was a right and a wrong and you could know on which side you were. And I just know that if I was working for NASA and I said that there were three answers: the space ship will hit the moon, the space ship will hit the sun or the space ship will just go off into Kingdom Come like in that film *2001 Whatitsname*, nobody would say, Excellent, well done, now take a guess at which one is the best shot. Like they would. Just at the end of the class my phone started to vibrate. It was this Sexual Groaning Sound because my bag was on the ground against the leg of the chair and the phone was vibrating against the leg. Everyone started to laugh. Peppa Pig, who is our Maths teacher, said: Turn that phone off. She looked straight at me. It took me five minutes at least to find it in my bag and it stopped and started to ring again. Sorry, Miss, sorry, Miss, sorry.

Then I saw it was my mam and I just knew. I started to cry. I'm just looking at the screen and it's still vibrating and I'm crying and everybody stops laughing.

So Serena had sex in Fuerteventura with an English boy a year younger than her. That's what she told me. She did it three times. When she came home she was sure she was pregnant because they didn't use condoms. Then it turned out she wasn't pregnant because she was on her period on the nail. By then she was bitching everyone and it was too late to change. She said she bitched people because she knew what they were going to say as soon as she started to show. I said to her I wouldn't have said anything.

Yeah, she said, like silence.

I said when Lauren O'Keefe had a baby I was the one who stayed friends with her.

That was just because you wanted to find out what it was like, you have a baby kink.

So yeah. I went through a phase where I was dreaming about being pregnant and having babies. I was like totally obsessed with it. I used to go to mother and baby websites and look up personal stories. But if you google it you'll find it's not as good as they say. Families of addiction. Your child is vaccine injured: a personal story. Cleft lip and cleft palate: a mother's story. Fragile X syndrome: one mother's story. Shaken baby syndrome. I was abandoned by my mother. One mother's personal tragedy. Secret thoughts of an abusive mother. I decided, considering my own family circumstances in which I can't stand to be in the same room as my mam, my dad is more or less a waste of space and my brother is weird, that I should give motherhood a miss. Because genetics. This was when I was fifteen and everything looked easy. I was all over Mumsnet reading about The Joys Of Pregnancy. I had reached Peak Baby. I even used the online Ovulation Calculator. Up until then I didn't even know I was ovulating. Like why would you ovulate if you're not married? Fifteen year olds are weird. When Serena was fifteen she used to think that 1D was better than the Beatles or even Def Leppard. I never listened to Def Leppard except I watched a couple of videos on YouTube just to see, but Serena says they are awesome. Tbh if Serena likes them they must be shit. Especially if 1D is better than them. Serena was and still probably is a Directioner. Except now she's undercover. Directioners are crazy. It's like a religion and they don't talk about it to Non-Directioners. It's like a secret cult. Like if you tell the secrets of Directioners you must die some horrible death.

My big mistake was telling Serena about the baby phase. I'd swear she had a little black book for stuff like that. A secret diary.

I wanted her to tell me about the sex but all she said was it was amazing.

Like, I totally expected it to be amazing but I wanted to know how it was amazing. She wouldn't tell me. She wouldn't even tell me if it hurt the first time. If you google *does losing my virginity hurt* you will get two hundred and thirty-one thousand hits. I asked her and she just looked stupid and said, Amaaaazing. When Serena puts on a Dreamy Look it's just a stupid face. I always want to punch her. She thinks it's Romantic. I try to tell her she looks like Miley Cyrus but with her tongue inside her mouth. She takes it as a compliment. I give up.

Sometimes Serena is so pale it looks like all you're seeing is the bone. Like one time I saw a human bone in a graveyard. I think it was human anyway. I didn't look at it for long. Maybe it was an animal, like a sheep bone idk. It was the colour of dirty chalk. That is Serena's face on those days. Maybe she is anaemic. Or constipated idk or maybe she doesn't sleep. History does not record.

My dad's heart attack went well. Or so I believe. He got a stent and they told him to stay away from work for a while. Which He Did Not Do. It's not that my dad does much work, it's just there's really nothing else in his life except driving around to look at places for sale, arguing with tenants and seeing solicitors about evictions. The evening he came home from hospital was one of those cold clear January days when it looks like the distance is made of glass. My mam drove him home. He looked thinner, paler, maybe a bit older too. Or just a bit angrier. I think he was angry at his heart for letting him down. My dad's heart has always been strong. Like he always thought he was some kind of Transformer, or like the droid in *Chappie*. I saw the trailer. It looks like crap. It's just boys are into machines killing things. Like Transformers. The autobots and the decepticons going for it like there was no tomorrow. That and calling each other cunts. I don't get it.

They also told him To Lose Weight. When I saw him in his pyjamas sitting up in one of those really narrow hospital beds I thought his belly would just pour out over the sides. How come I never noticed that happening? My dad is fat like in American TV shows. I blame Colonel Grace. My mam thinks KFC is a good way to feed a family of four. But maybe you get that way from sitting all day in a Lexus and only getting to tell people they are in breach of contract. Or maybe it's The Crash. Maybe it's the Revenge Of The Tenant. Or The Bank. In this country Banks are shit even at making money. Like what else is a bank for? Love and affection? Maybe my dad was always fat idk. Whatever, he is a tub of lard and it's surprising that his heart can even get up in the morning.

So he stayed home for a couple of weeks. He got his laptop and the portable phone. We had to keep the phone charged and eventually he got Mam to buy him a second one. I could hear his voice rumbling away all afternoon. I had to get the bus home so I didn't get back until after four. I would go up to his room and stick my head in. Hi, Dad. He would be on the phone. He would wave and sometimes smile. The properties of waves. Light is a wave but also a particle. Frequency, amplitude, period. There's always a fucking period. Every day, at school as it got closer to the last bell I would start to think, What if I find him dead? What if the stent fails? Or what if his heart just stops? What if I'm the one who finds him? So when he waved or smiled I would have to close the door fast in case I burst into tears. Sometimes even in the hallway, inside the front door, I could hear him talking.

During his recovery he evicted a Lithuanian couple.

Holly said a transplant might have been better than a stent.

Of course my mam didn't want Holly sleeping over. She said she had nits or lice or something. She said hippies are all the same. She said she was feckless and would end up pregnant at fourteen, even though she was already seventeen. None of it was true, but my mam just hated everything the Kellys stood for, whatever it was. Holly said it was just Capitalism against Anarchism and she didn't care. But she doesn't mind me sleeping in Holly's so that makes no sense. It was like catching nits or lice was a non-symmetric relation like in Maths when A *is related to* B and B *is related to* C but for some fucking reason that no one ever explained to me, A *is not related to* C. Like who would have thought. I would say my mam is racist except Holly is not ethnic. And my mam is Totally Racist when it comes to actual racism. She thinks immigrants are destroying the world. Holly says Capitalism is destroying the world. Serena says it's her parents and I say Whoever Is Destroying It Has Made A Good Job Of It.

Holly says I'm a Resistor. We did resistors in Physics. She sings that song about resistance being low. She teaches

61

me the words and we sing it together. I like the bit about keeping your distance because she can't really resist. I kinda feel like that about Holly.

Holly told me a story about a neighbour of hers who had a cat that liked hunting. One day the cat came home with the next-door neighbour's pet rabbit all covered in blood and muck. She panicked and gave the rabbit a wash and blow-dry and sneaked into the neighbour's garden and put the rabbit back in the hutch. This happened two more times. On the morning after the third event she met her neighbour. Something weird is happening, the neighbour said. My rabbit was knocked down by a car a few days ago but she has risen from her grave three times.

Holly thinks it's hilarious. She tried to tell it to Miss Leahy our Religion teacher. You can't escape Religion in my school. Even though Holly is a Conscientious Objector they make her sit in the back of the class and do her homework in case she might absorb holiness by osmosis. She says it is Subliminal Advertising. I googled it and she could be right.

Whatever. I caught my mother praying one night. She was kneeling against the couch with the *Bake Off* on mute. She had her hands joined like you see. I said, What are you doing, Mam? And she totally flipped out. She went from the prayer position to nuclear in one swift movement.

Your father has a heart attack and you JUST JUST carry on JESUS CHRIST I don't know where I got you,

you NEVER TIDY YOUR ROOM, look at you, DO
YOU HAVE ANY IDEA? YOUR FATHER NEARLY
DIED. JESUS CHRIST –

She didn't even stop when I backed out and closed
the door.

According to Miss Leahy religion is all about meaning. But get this: God created the world out of chaos, then he created man, then he organised the days of the week so that Sunday was boring af, then he had the Jews faffing about trying to find the Promised Land which turns out to be Palestine which is an excuse to kill Palestinians, then he sent his own son to be crucified like you do, then he encouraged his true believers to crucify a lot of other people to save their souls, then finally we get Sunday Mass, The Blessed Sacrament, Forgiveness Of Sins, The Parish Fucking Priest, The Pope, Michelangelo, The Sacrament Of Marriage, The Assumption Of The Blessed Virgin Into Heaven and Giving Up Sweets For Lent. If I ever saw a completely fucking random get-up, this is it. Like he should have left it at chaos. If God was the CEO of a Fortune 500 company he would be toast by now. Come to think of it, maybe he'd just be a billionaire and making a major contribution to Global Warming and the Extinction Of Planet Earth aka Armageddon. Which is kind of cool, when you think about it; chaos coming again. Come back, God, all is forgiven lol.

Actually I think Armageddon is an actual God thing from the Bible idk I should google it but I'm like totally cya.

Serena doesn't like Holly. She tells me things she thinks I don't know. Like Holly Had A Urinary Tract Infection in second year and according to Serena It Was Because She Was Having Dirty Sex. I told her I already knew about it and it wasn't sex just some infection. Serena thinks that's hilarious. Or she pretends she does. She's studying all the news reports about the Graham Dwyer trial. She has googled them all. She has screenshots. She wants to talk about what it would feel like to be completely in the power of a man.

I say: Try my dad.

Serena puts on the concerned medical professional face. How is your poor dad?

He's in the recovery position, I say. If he obeys orders he'll be fine.

I worry about him, she says.

Like totally randomly she's worrying about my dad. She has her own dad to worry about and frankly if I was her I'd be worried just being in the same house as him.

She tells me that Holly's dad did time in prison. She's wondering if doing time in prison makes you a dominant. Less like a dominant I never met. Holly's dad is a total pussycat. Serena doesn't know why he was in prison, but I do and I won't tell her. I pretend it's a mystery. For a while we make up things he might have done. Serena's favourite is some kind of murder – with knives or an axe. I point out that you don't get out in under a year for an axe murder. Her second fave is pyromaniac. That's because she likes fires. When we were kids she used to light fires in a part of her garden where she couldn't be seen. They have this huge garden with a glasshouse and a boathouse (disused) at the bottom and a view over the sea. They have a see-saw and a climbing frame. They have a paddling pool (disused). We used to say we were experimenting with how different things burned. She even started to get petrol out of her mother's car using a tube and a bottle. She watched YouTube videos of people throwing petrol bombs during riots. I know an OCD when I see one believe me.

Serena has a dinosaur onesie, like with dinosaur-coloured scales on the back and a tail. The hoodie has a sort of head on it. With a beak and eyes. It is the scariest thing you could possibly wake up to. I always sleep in my T-shirt and panties but because I'm sharing a bed with Serena I wear my jammies. So we get in and turn the light out. I'm really tired but Serena wants to talk about my dad's heart attack and his stent. She found an amaaaazing video of open heart surgery. You can see the heart beating. It's an operation in India and all the doctors and nurses are Indian. I said I imagined the patient was Indian too and she said you couldn't see because he was all covered in green cloth. I said I was joking and she bitch-slapped me on the shoulder, not hard because she was lying beside me. And they had a big square hole in the chest with a set square or something to measure it. And everybody was totally cool like it was someone cutting up a chicken.

I said I didn't want to know but she kept going. Serena is psycho, like if you look up psycho on Wikipedia you're looking at a description of Serena. She has NO empathy with another human being. Or an animal. She has no idea what goes on in someone else's head.

I said: Serena, my dad had a fucking heart attack, OK? Like the whole Ballyshane thing nearly killed him. I don't want to know about the inside of his heart? OK?

So then she noticed I was shaking and she was all over me. She started FUCKING HUGGING ME and calling me BABY. Jesus wept twice.

I sat up. I said, Serena, I just want to go to sleep. I don't want to know what the inside of my dad's fucking chest looks like. So drop it, OK?

She rolled over onto her side and pretended to be falling asleep. So I did the same. After like three minutes she said, Are you really a lezzer?

Go to sleep.

Like, I'm wondering what it's like. Is it like sex?

Well, I said, you don't get a dick inside you...

So you are.

She sat up again. I knew it, I fucking knew it. Who did you do? Was it Holly? Of course it was Holly, who else for fuck's sake. What's she like?

Serena, if you google lesbian porn you will see that they don't have dicks.

Except for strap-ons.

They're strap-ons not dicks.

So you're not lesbian? Yes or no? I have to know.

Why?

Because I want to try it.

Well don't fucking try it on me. Stay in that fucking dinosaur or I'll kill you I swear.

Now silence. Now she's pouting. Like I'm supposed to have Rejected Her Advances. At times like this I see why she has no friends. Like why did I invite her to sleep over? Idk. It must have been a moment of weakness. If I remembered the dinosaur I certainly wouldn't have done it.

So I tell her about my dad and his obsession and I know I'm making a mistake before I have said five sentences. But still I tell her. It's three in the morning and it all pours out. I even tell her about the fanlight over the door. And I tell her I think hating this Tom Bowles guy gave my dad his heart attack. And after a while I feel this dinosaur paw holding my hand and that's just it. We just lie there and talk properly. And it turns out that she admires my dad and she thinks I'm so lucky, and it must be lovely to have a dad who understands, and I should love him better, and other strange crap. Like, He's so handsome. But I'm worried about him more or less permanently, so I just lie there in the dark and maybe cry sometimes idk it's just he nearly died. So. And sometime around four o'clock we fall asleep and we wake still holding hands. Who knew dinosaurs had hearts? I wake before her and I look at her and she's beautiful in sleep. All that craziness and bitchiness and spite is gone. I think, Serena would make a beautiful corpse. I can even see her in a coffin. If I could I would bury her in her dinosaur onesie.

So now she has a new idea. She wants us to go up to Ballyshane in the middle of the night and scare the people. She wants to buy crow-bangers or fireworks or light a fire. First of all, I say, how are we going to sneak out of this house? My dad is a light sleeper. Even when I go to the toilet he knows. Secondly, what's the point? Thirdly, no way am I lighting any fires like she can do her pyromania stuff on her own. Same difference for thieving. And she can forget about the fireworks and bangers, I have too much respect for my life. She says I'm just a pussy and we have a good laugh about that. It's the first good laugh we've had since we got back together and it feels nice. Like Serena is not the worst. Idk. And she says, Your dad is out of it, he's on painkillers and antibiotics and shit, he won't wake! Then we started looking at old photos in my desk drawer, like actual printed photos, and Serena found my First Year copybook and we had a good laugh about the kind of homework we got which we thought was way too much. Back in the day. Like if it took half an hour it was unfair. Now we devote our life to homework. It's like the thing we did in Religion about the season for all things and this is the Fucking Season For Homework. Jesus fuck my life.

Story for English. My Exciting Discovery
Suzy Regan First Year

My name is Doctor Johansen and I am a professor. I found an exciting discovery forty years ago. It was the skeleton of a little girl. It was three point two million years old! That is a record for the oldest child ever discovered.

I was working on a archaological dig in Afar, Africa and that day wasn't going too well. It was very hot and I was real thirsty and we weren't finding things. We looked everywhere but there was nothing. So I was thinking of giving up and just writing something when I thought 'Why not go over the place again.'

It was then I decided that the dried up river might be a good place. Even though guys already done it. I went down there and had a walk and took a good look around. To my surprise there was a bit of a skeleton sticking out of the mud. It was a elbow.

Then I started digging and I found a bit of her skull and other stuff. I was really excited. I called all my friends and we got her out. We were really happy because we knew she was three point two million years old. How we knew that was we knew that was how old the mud was.

So that night we had a campfire and a bit of a sing-song and someone sang the Beetles hit Lucy In the Sky With Diamonds. And I said that's what we'll call her, Lucy. And that is how she came to be named. She was forty per cent complete, which is a lot for a three point two million year old person. I got famous then because I disocvered her. Now i am a professor and I have a good job. And it is all down to finding Lucy. She was the most exciting discovery of my life.

So we set a fire. It was not a big fire. And it did not go well. It happened a night Serena was sleeping over again. My mam was happy that Serena and me were back together again because Serena's father is idk a surgeon of some kind maybe eyes and my mam is impressed by that. My dad is impressed too but he never says anything. Like doctors are gods in this country. She even bought us a Chinese to eat in my room. I hate the smell of ex-Chinese food. Or Chinese ex-food. The sweety-soury smell. I like noodles though. And crispy duck is ace.

We consumed the Chinese. Or I consumed it and Serena had some noodles. Like maybe four. We listened to music with one earphone each (Serena's set fell into the toilet and she flushed it because it was ew), watched a movie, *Love Actually*. My third time. But watching it with Serena is hell. She can tell me that the CD track that Karen is listening to when she's crying is track 7 – she pauses it to show me – but the correct track on the correct Joni Mitchell CD is like 12 or something, and time goes backwards when Sarah and Karl are in the bedroom according to the bedside clock, and when David goes to Downing Street his tie keeps changing between scenes, stuff like that. I like Joni Mitchell but I'd say Serena has never even heard her. Serena totally ruined *Love Actually*. Then we took selfies in various poses. And basically we waited until three in the morning because Serena said nobody wakes up between three and four. Except I know my dad often goes for a pee around four. Except since his operation he has been out of it on drugs, so he holds on to it until Mam wakes him. I wish I had some of what he's taking.

To stay awake we made up names of books for porn: *Hard Time* by Nobby DickIn, and the sequel *Harder Time*, *Knobhanger Alley* by Jane AssTon, *CurlyOldAnus* by William ShagsPair. Then we told jokes. When we ran out of jokes we googled them. Some interesting ones turned up. Like I didn't know that strap-on backwards is no-parts. It's easy to stay awake when you want to sleep but when you want to stay awake you keep falling asleep. Then we watched Creepy YouTube Videos with the Sound Off. Serena practically has her own channel. She majors in Shit That Makes Me Sick. The creepiest was one called Crooked Rot which featured a Play-Doh head with a bloody tube going into its brain. I swear. I had to close my eyes. Then there were ones about squeezing pimples. Idk. Serena worries me, she really does. But then I worry me too.

She told me she registered with alt.com. She showed it to me. It had a photo of a girl with a dog's collar and the leash in her hand. The girl's cheeks were blushing. She was naked. The text said: Find who shares your kinks, 1,186,040 Active Members. Join For Free. Her username was *Hrt.me.Hrt.me*. She wanted to click Login but I said, Enough already. It's time to go. She went. I'm guessing that the fire kink was stronger than whatever she had going on alt.com.

We got dressed and went downstairs. I already disabled the alarm just after Mam and Dad went to bed. I pretended I was just checking that it was on. I'm slightly paranoid, so…

Outside we walked on the grass not the gravel. My dad imported the gravel from The Isle Of Wight. It is this incredible golden-brown colour and I googled it and it's practically an endangered species, they have to scoop it up from the bottom of the English Channel. It is one of the stand-out features of our property, if we ever went to sell it, a gravel feature. Like we also have a pond feature and a gazebo feature and in the sitting room we have a fireplace feature. I get to read all the property specs while I'm driving home with Dad. It's all he has to read.

We didn't walk on the gravel feature because it makes a sound.

The grass was crispy af from frost.

I said, It's going to be cold up Ballyshane.

I don't know why but I was suddenly hungry. I could murder for an apple turnover.

Ballyshane actually looks down on my house. Or my house looks up at it – you can see the first floor windows if our bathroom window is open. The bathroom window is frosted glass even though we don't have any neighbours. In case of peeping toms I suppose. Idk. Someone who would come all the way out here and hide in the gazebo feature to watch us undressing for a shower or peeing. I wish. My mam said she couldn't do a pee with clear glass. Even though it's like the universal bathroom not their en suite. So she wouldn't have to. They decided not to put an en-suite in every room when they built the place even though it enhances the value. I don't know why. I would like to be able to look out when I'm doing mine, but I can only do it in the summer time when it's hot and we leave all the windows open. And if my mam walks in she says, Shut that!

Serena had a ten per cent extra cleanser bottle full of petrol. It was plastic and she thought the petrol was dissolving it. It was also rock-hard and blown up like a balloon. I think the petrol got warmed up in my room. It might have exploded which would totally ruin my carpet. I didn't know she had it. She said it was for me. Like I would want a mini petrol bomb sitting in her little overnight bag with a special inset for makeup and a mirror. Maybe she always travels with a petrol bomb. Serena is quite capable.

It was freezing. Like freeze your boobs off cold. Like frostbite your arse off cold. By the time we got to Ballyshane the cleanser bottle was soft again. A bit squishy even, idk maybe she was right and the petrol was eating it. There was some crazy bird singing somewhere. Maybe a blackbird or something. I wondered if birds got

77

high if they ate something. Like fermented berries and stuff. Or magic mushrooms idk if birds eat mushrooms. History does not record.

All the lights were out.

Which was not surprising, it was four thirty more or less.

We went all around the house. It was totally cool being able to look in all the windows. It was very tidy. There was this one room which was old Corry's study and it was full of books still. It looked like this Bowles dude bought everything. If he was such a hot-shot writer why didn't he bring his own? Writers are always doing selfies in rooms full of books, I remember one of the late Seamus Heaney who is on our course and there were books falling off the table and stacks on the floor, like did he even read some of them? He is boring. We did 'Digging' in Primary and then we had to do it again when I came to Secondary, like three times because we changed English teachers. If fucking digging was so much fun how come he didn't become a builder instead of a poet? He could be putting in foundations. And the one about his midterm break. I have a cousin in England she even did that one.

The moon was shining on that side of the house, a big rough piece of bone in a black box. The next window was the kitchen. It was the same higgledy piggledy Formica stuff, like you'd see in old people's houses. Not built in at all. Like my grandad's house was all over the place too.

We couldn't work out how we might attract their attention to the fire until Serena got the idea of setting the alarm off. So that decided us to set the fire outside the drawing room window because we could see a wire and some kind of a sensor on the glass. Like old Miss Corry always called it the drawing room. So we would set the fire, wait until it was blazing and then give the window a thump and run for the trees.

The plan didn't come together.

First we couldn't find anything to burn. Serena started to complain that the petrol was leaking through the plastic so we put it down and then we couldn't find where we put it. It took ten minutes to find it in the dark. Eventually we found the recycling bin and there was cardboard in it. Then we decided to make the fire in the bin. It was a plastic bin so that was good because it would burn too. But Serena knew we needed something a bit heavier. So we went into the trees and tried to break some branches off. They just bent. What kind of trees they were meant to be idk. Luckily we found a couple of bits that fell down sometime. One was heavy enough that two of us had to carry it. We got it into the bin. It was a wheelie bin. All our bins are. So we rolled the whole thing over the lawn to the drawing room window. I checked my phone and it was already well after five. I was starting to get worried that we'd get caught getting back in.

So we got the bin in place with the log sticking up in the cardboard. Serena opened the cleanser bottle and poured it in and I lit the match and dropped it in. But it went out. I threw another one. Same difference. Serena said it's the cold that's putting it out.

We have to light it inside the bin.

No fucking way, I said. Like the fumes. Like whoosh. No fucking way.

And she's like: I'm gonna do it, Suzy, I'm gonna do it, baby.

She took the matchbox and sort of hunched over the bin. I saw the flare of the match. I closed my eyes. I knew I would hear a whoosh and then I'd know that Serena the fucking dinosaur had set fire to herself. But all I heard was Serena saying, Fuck fuck fuck.

The match went out again.

Jesus, this is pathetic, I said.

Serena just looked at me.

I said, We're going to end up pulling the bin all the way back to where we got it and then we'll have to put the branch back. And someone'll come out tomorrow and they'll get the smell of petrol from the bin. Like fuck's sake.

Serena struck another match and put her hand right in and it went out on the way down. Her hand was shaking.

Wait, I said. Take out a piece of cardboard, dry stuff with no petrol. We'll light it outside.

So we fished out a piece of cardboard and huddled it and the third match lit it. And we stayed huddled until it was well burning, then Serena lowered it into the bin. At the last minute she panicked and dropped it, but it stayed lighting in one corner. And then it started to burn and then there was a whoosh and the petrol caught. We got back fast enough. But I could smell burnt hair. We high-fived twice. We were laughing. The petrol was burned out now, but the cardboard was up and some plastic water bottles and bits of twigs were beginning to light. And smoke was starting, black horrible smoke. And the whole circa two hundred acres/circa eighty hectares was going to fill up with our polluted poison smoke. Suddenly I just thought this was a bad idea from the start, how did I ever go along with it?

I backed away but Serena stayed. She was standing sideways to me. Her face was the same as that morning I woke up and she was asleep beside me in her dinosaur onesie. Now I knew the word for it: serene. She was serene and the flames glowed in her eyes. Serena Serene, Serene Serena. It was beautiful. Maybe like something from *Clash of the Titans*. I took a shot of her standing like that but the flash is off and when I looked at it afterwards all you could see was a red glow from the bin and something like the ghost of Serena on the edge.

Serena, Serena, I whispered. We need to stop.

She looked at me. She was out of it. The fire idk took hold of her or something. She was in an altered state.

We need to go, I said, we'll get caught getting back. And they might see the fire.

She grinned. Then she turned and ran at the window. She sort of just totally threw herself at it. She actually broke it but it didn't shatter. A lightning down

81

the middle. I could see it. She was probably expecting double-glazing but it must have been strong glass anyway. Old guys' houses like this never have double-glazing. And a bell started to ring. Like a totally old bell, like something from a film about an old prison. I shouted to Serena and I ran. When I got to the trees she wasn't with me. I looked back at the fire but she wasn't there either. There was a light in the room with the broken window and I could see the old guy and someone else behind, maybe the housekeeper. The bin was melting and losing shape. It was slowly turning into a blob. The smoke was terrible. The wind was blowing in my direction and I could feel my throat closing against it. A light was on in an upstairs room.

Fuck you, Serena, I said.

I couldn't see her.

I ran again. This time I went as far as the road. Then I thought they would have called the guards and the guards would come by the road. FFS. I would have to go home across the fields and the moon was down behind clouds. I decided to take a chance on the road and if a cop car came I would see the headlights in time. I ran all the way home. Serena wasn't there.

My dad freaked. Legit he went purple in the face. I thought he would have another heart attack. The Dog went back to his basket. He just puts his head down when people shout. I was thinking oh fuck oh fuck. My dad is going to die because I did some pyromania with Serena. Like I googled stents and they can fail. And where was Serena? And my dad was saying how dare I leave the house in secret like that, and who was I seeing, and I was trying to say I felt bad and went for a walk to clear my head, and my dad said, What's that smell? And I said, stupidly, I thought I saw smoke up at Ballyshane, I might be wrong. And suddenly my dad went upstairs and opened the bathroom window. And you couldn't see anything.

Well, you could see lights.

There's no fucking fire anyway, my dad said. But all their lights are on.

He closed the blinds again.

I don't want you sneaking out of the house, miss, my dad said.

No, Dad. It was just this once. Look my boots are filthy from the fields.

He looked at my boots.

Take your boots off and don't be traipsing it all over the house, will you look at the state of that floor!

OK, Dad, sorry.

And stop shouting or you'll wake your mother.

Sorry.

Stop saying sorry.

I took my boots off and wrapped them in toilet paper. I should have used kitchen towel. Dad decided to go back to bed. I said, See you, Dad. I went into my room and closed the door and very fast tucked some pillows into the bed to make it look like there was someone in there. Then I undressed and got in. I was thinking, This is so random, where is Serena, what's going to happen when they find out, I don't believe this is happening. And what was my dad doing awake at that hour walking around in his old-guy pyjamas?

Then I heard him go downstairs. I heard him go out. I heard the car move off doing its best to stay quiet. My dad making a mysterious getaway in the dark of night. Maybe he couldn't sleep idk maybe there was a house for sale and he wanted to be first in the queue.

It was half past five when I heard someone throwing things at my window. I knew who it was. Like it wasn't fucking Catherine Linton née Earnshaw. I sneaked downstairs, and turned off the alarm. She was outside on the step. I made her take her boots off and we got back to my room. As soon as we got inside the door we hugged so bad it was like we were never going to let go. She was shaking and her skin was totally icy cold. I helped her get her clothes off and into her onesie and then we got back into bed. She was shivering like crazy and crying and I tried to calm her down and warm her up at the same time. I had the feeling as I undressed her that she wanted to tell me something. She kept giving me puppy-dog eyes and biting her lip and stuff idk I just thought maybe there was a reveal coming. I just hoped she wasn't going to declare her undying love for me or something else embarrassing.

But I had time to see the cuts on her thigh. I never knew about that. Little red slashes, some crossed. I didn't say anything.

To everyone's surprise except me, my brother broke up
with his girlfriend. I don't know why. It cast a gloom
over the entire family including The Dog. But Not Me.
My dad was eyeing that Audi dealership her father had.
And my mam drives Audi. All that Vorsprung durch
Technik. Whatever that means. But it's in German so it
must be good right? The German teachers in my school
are all Nazis. You hear them screaming because someone
forgot part of her uniform. Like her tie. Why do girls
have to wear ties anyway? She said to Holly: Rules are
rules, and we all agree to the rules so you must obey. Like
who agreed? Miss Philpott would send you to the gas
chambers for not having a tie or for tucking your skirt
up into the waist to make a mini. Mr Leary made a joke
once upon a time about Hitler's speech at Nuremberg,
like we did a case study on the Nuremberg Rallies. We
were listening to Miss Philpott next door freaking about
something. He sort of brushed his hair the way Hitler
did and made a moustache with his finger and with
the other hand he did the chopping-like gestures that
old Adolf was so fond of and said, Ze uniform Nazis
vill be holding a rally lader to check if the mädchens

are vearing their knickerz. We all giggled, not because it was funny, which nothing Leary does is, but because Leary said knickers. Leary is all right. The next week he showed us a bit of this film about Nuremberg and sure enough they had the same uniform as us. Well, it was black and white. And we have a German girl in my school and she's really chilled and when she hears Miss Philpott doing her Hitler thing she's like, What the absolute fuck? Except in a real German accent. I didn't tell anyone my brother's girlfriend was allowing hate messages about him on her Facebook page. And my dad got into some kind of trouble idk. I came home from school after a shit day and I heard my mam shouting at him in the bedroom. She was saying, You stupid, stupid man, you thick bastard, Jesus Christ, did you think you'd get away with it? More stuff like that.

So I took The Dog out for a walk. I think he was surprised but he liked it anyway. He wanted to go down Regan's Glen and he's the boss. I let him snuffle along the furze clumps and the riverbank. He had fun. He is always hoping for a rat. I was thinking of the time my dad took me for a spin and we ended up at one of the houses he owns in some Avenue or Close or Paddock or Drive called after some godforsaken English village like all of ours are, and there was a woman there with a new baby. I don't know what we were doing there. She was nice and the baby was adorable, a little fat Tupac, like when he was bald. Not as black though. More brown. The mother was brown too. She had a long neck. Not just a long neck but like a swan, a brown swan. She was beautiful. Her eyes were comforting. When she looked at me I thought she loved me. I always go for the eyes first.

I asked my dad afterwards.

What was that about, Dad?

I wanted you to meet her.

Why?

She's a nice person.

I thought about that. My dad never brought me to see a nice person before. For all I know all the people he didn't evict out of our houses might have been nice people. But he brought me to see this one person. True, she was nice. And she had a baby and babies are irresistible. And I couldn't see any man things around the place. And my dad made her tea like he knew his way around the kitchen. Well, we own the kitchen. Some kind of special tea, Lapsang thingy. And she didn't even say, I'll do it, like my mam would. She let him make it. And bring it out. And my dad even cuddled the baby. I have never seen my dad cuddle anybody especially a baby. The closest is I saw him put his arms around a horse's neck once.

So, I said, what's the story about the baby?

He shrugged. The father went back to Africa.

Africa is a continent, Dad. What part of Africa?

Nigeria I think.

Dad, Nigerians are real black, like black black. If you mix a brown person with a black person you get a baby who is browny-black. This baby is the other way. Like the baby is only off-white or something.

I was thinking that if I had John Brown's baby he would have been that colour. A beautiful oily brown like some kind of dress fabric, like satin or something. My mam has a tan satin blouse. It would be like that. It gave me a warm feeling just to think about having John Brown's baby, but it made me sad too. Because I will never get him back. Even though he wasn't mine ever. I just liked being near him.

That's all genetics stuff, he said, you never know what way someone's skin will go. I'll tell you something for nothing, Suzy, sometimes two white people get a black baby. And anyway not all Nigerians are that black. She has Irish citizenship and so has the baby.

Cool.

She was born in Morocco or someplace.

And how old is she now?

My dad looked away. Look at that fucker, he said.

A man was trying to reverse a forklift out of some kind of a factory or warehouse and he backed it straight into a parked car. We drove past. There was no one in the car. The guy in the forklift was scratching his head. I looked back. He made shit of the door and the passenger side mirror. My dad was still saying nothing.

Does she pay her rent, Dad?

He nodded.

Like if she didn't pay her rent my dad is Conan the Barbarian. No prisoners taken. It's just his way. No arrears, no deposit back until the cutlery is counted and the bills come in marked paid and the accounts closed. On the other side of it, if someone rings up and says there's a leak in the roof or the toilet is blocked, he's on to it. Joe Daly is his man. Joe Daly fixes everything. And Joe has Piotr, a Polish guy and there's a Latvian what his name is Idk. They do our garden. Mam says they're butchers but Dad says they keep it clean and tidy. Nothing much grows in it except blackbirds and finches and grass.

So I was thinking about the black lady and watching The Dog snuffling along the river bank. Her name is Sarah. I was just standing there in the middle of this rough field in the shelter of a furze bush when I noticed something in The Dog's mouth. It was a purse. I took it from him. I had to slap him on the nose to get it. It was a cheap purse and there was money in it and a mascara tube and other stuff and a pack of Durex Tingle Me with Minty Lube for a Tingly Sensation. It was a twelve pack and just for fun I counted them and there were twelve. The twelve apostles. I thought about keeping a few and then I thought what if there's a body in the furze and this is evidence? It would be evidence tampering. All the programmes are very strong about evidence tampering, like *The Wire* and idk detective thingies. I dropped the purse. I walked all around the furze clump trying to see in. When I got back to where I dropped the purse it was gone.

My face just went cold from the top down. I started to shake. There was no house that could see into Regan's Glen. Where I was standing you couldn't even see the road.

I started to call The Dog. I tried to whistle but my lips were too hard. My throat was dry.

I ran around the furze.

Like idk why I ran around the furze. There was nothing there.

Then I saw The Dog with the purse. He was lying down eating it. He was down by the stream. I ran down but he ran away. I ran after him. It was getting dark and he was too fast. So I pretended I was going home. I whistled and this time my lips worked. I watched him out of the corner of my eye. After a while he turned up to come home with me with his tail wagging. Like I'm supposed to be pleased to see him. He was probably thinking of his dinner. I grabbed him by the collar and went back down the field to find the purse. I couldn't find it. I even thought I should let him go and see if he'd find it but I knew he'd do a runner again. I could have sworn I knew exactly where he was eating it last. But it was gone. And it was dark. I went home. I was thinking I should phone the guards. Who throws away a purse with money in it?

This evening my mam was watching telly. She had a glass of wine. She drinks Sancerre. I've had some. It's not bad. It's a sort of high-class Chardonnay. Tbf I don't like wine, but Sancerre is ok. It's French. They must know something about making wine they've been at it for a while. I said, Everything OK, Mam? She said, Yep, your chop is in the oven and oven chips. I was thinking, if my dad just confessed that he had a love child by a Moroccan lady, she was taking it pretty cool. Maybe I was wrong. So I told her about the purse. She said ring the guards. Tomorrow was Saturday. Maybe somebody reported it missing.

So I rang the station. Guards are thick.

Guard: Could you put your mammy on the phone for me?

Me: She's watching *The Great British Bake Off*. She never misses it. Or *Master Chef*. Like foodie programmes are trending in my house big time.

Guard: Is there any witness to this?

Me: Like The Dog?

Guard: Did you tell anyone? Your mammy and daddy?

Me: My mam told me to ring.

Guard: Why didn't you bring the purse with you?

Me: The Dog took it, like it was nearly dark, he wanted to eat it, you know, dogs. And then I couldn't find it.

Guard: Why did you give it to the dog?

Me: He took it. I didn't give it to him.

Guard: Did you notice any contents?

I blushed but he couldn't see through the phone. There was a mascara…

Guard: A mascara… Is that like make-up?

Me: A tube thingy. For eye make-up.

Guard: A tube…

Me: A wallet…

Guard: Any money?

Me: A good bit. A few fifties at least. I didn't count it though.

Guard: That's a lot of money to leave lying around a field now.

Me: And a packet of…

Guard: A packet of…

I took a deep breath. Durex Tingle Me.

There was a long silence. Then: Durex what?

Me: Never mind.

Guard: Could you repeat that, Miss?

Me: A packet of fucking condoms, right?

Guard: I'll put a packet of condoms down.

Me: Right. A twelve pack.

Guard: Anything else?

Me: There was other stuff. I don't remember.

Guard: I'll put, and several other unidentified items.

Me: Right.

Guard: And the location again?

Me: Regan's Glen.

Guard: Exactly. I know where that is. It's a long old glen though. Still, if someone comes in about the purse we'll be able to jog her memory. Now thanks for reporting that so. You're a good girl.

Me: But what about if someone was murdered?

Guard: Ah now, if someone was murdered sure we'd know about it. Missing persons and that. We get told. But if someone turns up dead, we'll call you back. Did I get your mobile? I did. I have it here. Good night now, love. Take care, byebyebye.

My mam asked me what was in the purse. It was still the *Bake Off*. I told her. I didn't mention the condoms – once was enough. She whistled. Well, it's not whistling, she can't whistle. It's a sort of whistling sound she does in the gap between her two front teeth. But like, she's sucking the air in not blowing it out. It's not technically whistling unless it's coming out.

Mam: That's a lot of money.

Me: That's what the cop said.

Mam: Guard.

Me: That's what the guard said.

Mam: Don't call him cop.

Me: I won't.

Mam: They're guards.

Me: I know.

Mam: Did you eat your chop?

Me: I did.

Mam: For once. If I see it in the bin I'll slaughter you.

Me: I ate it. I was hungry. Like I eat food, it's just KFC. It's not real.

Mam: You'll eat what's put in front of you, my lassie.

Me: What were you shouting at Dad about?

Mam: None of your business. It's a business problem.

These are the times when I hate her. When she's sat there like some kind of expert on everything and whatever happens I'm wrong. I know nothing. I do nothing right. And at the same time I don't exist. Not by comparison with the *Bake Off*. Which is considering the question of some kind of yeast.

She stared at the telly for a minute then she said, There's a homeless guy sleeping in Avondale Close. Dad is trying to get the Simon to take responsibility for him. That's what they're for, isn't it? Homeless shelters. They don't give a shit really, quite frankly. They're a waste of taxpayers' money.

Me: I thought you were getting divorced.

I used to think I would die if they got divorced but just now I was hoping they would, except for what it would do to my dad. It would save me killing her and getting a life sentence for matricide. You never get away with that kind of thing.

She gave me one of her looks. Like she's thinking, Where did I get this child? Now the telly was saying Text BAKE to 70005. That's the end. My mam never texts BAKE. She flicked the remote. Channels started to come up one after the other. I don't know how many channels we have but I know you get the porn ads right out towards the end and you better have the mute on. I went to my room.

And of course the very next morning there was a murder in the news. The guards rang me in school. Could I take them back to the spot? It was the same guard. It turns out he was thinking of a different glen altogether. They would send a squad car. It was a dead woman and she was found inside the wall of Ballyshane, that's the old wall that was built during the famine. Ballyshane did well out of the famine. The sale of the house did not comprise it because the farm was sold separately. Gardaí had sealed off the area and were awaiting the arrival of the Assistant Chief State Pathologist from Dublin. I would like to be a pathologist. They are always so cool. And nothing psychs them out. And you only have to talk to dead people and detectives. And maybe a creepy assistant. And you go into court and say only what you found, exactly that and nothing else. You can say yes and no at the same time. Yes, it's possible, no it's not likely. I can't possibly say. May it please the court. The cuts on her thighs might have been self-inflicted or they might have been the result of a struggle. The blood on her dinosaur onesie was not her own. It's impossible to say. The attacker was left-handed.

The squad car arrived at small break. Nobody knew the guards were coming for me. It felt great.

But the back seat smelled like vomit. It was ew. I tried to see where I shouldn't sit but it was all gross. Don't they get them cleaned? The passenger was a girl guard. She was a blonde and totally pretty. I expected that there would be banter like you see, but herself and the fat driver said nothing the whole time except, Where to now? Left or Right? Here?

We walked down the glen. It wasn't too cold. There was a magpie swaggering around like a rugby player in a neoprene vest. He looked like he was sneering at us. Magpies are sneery birds. There was a mist but it was melting or whatever it does. The sun was nice. I showed them where The Dog found it, then we walked around a lot. I stayed with the girl. Her eyes were an amazing pale blue and she had a dimple on each side of her mouth. I would say she worked out. I asked her what it was like being a guard. She said, It was OK, but sometimes it was shit, like all jobs, you get good days and bad days. Her name was Sharon.

We found the purse. It was so cool, they had those plastic gloves like you see. I told them that I went through it with my bare hands and they said I would have to be fingerprinted to eliminate my prints. So cool. Serena would just die. Holly didn't like the guards so she'd be like so what. But I could see myself being fingerprinted and getting my mugshot. Would they give me a copy to take home? Like, Hi Serena, want to see my fingerprints and mugshot and stuff?

They looked in and found the card and they looked at each other.

That's her, the Guard said.

Right, Sharon said to me, back to the car, this is a crime scene now.

I was like in heaven. Me at a crime scene. I wanted to take a selfie but I didn't think it would be allowed. It would be a hit on Facebook.

They'd be taking a statement from me, Sharon said. She was the higher-up, it looked like, which was a surprise. The fat guard was older than her.

The guards dropped me home and the first phone call I got was exactly at the end of school from Serena. Like LOL. What happened? I saw you going away in a squad car? OMG. The murder! The MURDER!

And later I found out the woman was killed somewhere and all her stuff and her clothes were taken and they were searching the area for a radius of miles and asking for anyone with information that might be relevant to come forward, and it turned out that her body was badly cut up, according to a neighbour of a friend of the man who found her, blood everywhere and stark naked. The neighbour of the friend of the man said she was hot too. Which, when you come to think of it, is weird af. Saying it, I mean. Or even thinking it. He was out walking the dog. It is always dog-owners who find dead bodies, which is one of the reasons I am Totally Not Keen On Walking The Dog In Lonely Places. But in a way The Dog walks me. I always expected a body, I just ended up finding the purse instead.

So, we went to a birthday party. We didn't know it would be a free gaff and the boys would all be tanked. It was bad. Like I mean bad idk very bad. We didn't know any of them. They had stuff in small bottles. One of them had a hip flask. Serena danced me first and then Holly and then Serena danced the boy with the hip flask and then they disappeared. Another boy danced me and he was all hands. I had to tell him to take his hands off my arse. He was not a happy camper. He went off in a sulk in the middle of the number. I saw him talking to other boys and looking at me. I made up my mind to stick with Holly for the rest of the night. I didn't want to find myself upstairs with a gang of them. I wanted to go home but we couldn't go without Serena. It was Serena was invited. Two boys asked me to go outside. One after the other. No fucking way. They were those big guys, like rugby or something, with necks like those long balloons you see. I don't even like that kind of body. And they're generally stupid too. I told the second guy I was underage and he started to laugh like it was a joke.

About an hour later Serena turned up again and she said she wanted to go home. Holly and I were just beginning to enjoy ourselves, we were dancing together, and we were idk pissed about it or something, because we said no, she'd have to wait. So she went somewhere. And at eleven thirty the birthday girl's parents came home unexpectedly and that was really the end of that, even though some of us stayed around for a bit to be polite. Holly said they were proper buffers. It was all young lady this and young lady that. So then we had to call somebody's dad to come and collect us and Serena's dad was on call so he couldn't come. And so it ended up that Holly's dad came out for us in his ancient Toyota. Serena said the car smelled of dog shit. She didn't want to get in. I don't think Holly heard. Holly was telling her dad about the guys with the naggins of whiskey. Then she said about the guy with the hip flask and her Dad said something I didn't hear and Holly laughed and Serena leaned against me and whispered in my ear, I was upstairs with him, I let him do it. I said, Did you use anything? She said, I think he loves me. I said, Did he say that before or after?

She didn't talk to me the rest of the way home. We took a strange route idk it seemed to take twice as long. And that road brought us back past Ballyshane. By then Serena was asleep with her head on my shoulder.

What I saw passing Ballyshane was my father's car stopped at a place where you could look at the house through the trees. I couldn't see who was in it because we went past too quickly, but when I got home the car was gone. I went to bed. Sometimes in my bed, once everyone is asleep, I kinda start to think that everything is different to what I see. That it's like the way light leaves a block of glass. In Physics you see how the light makes an angle θ with the inside surface of the glass block and a completely different angle out in the air. Like everything is going one way inside and whenever I get out into the air it'll be going a different direction. Or like if I could walk out backwards I would be with my real family, the one I actually belong to, where we all love each other or something. And everyone would be normal. I was trying not to think about Serena and Hip Flask Guy, but about one o'clock she started texting me. The first thing she said was, OML we didn't use anthing ☹. Serena has autocorrect turned off. I just replied: IKR night now. I did not sleep. It was a Saturday night. He didn't have a condom with him and she didn't have one. Anyway he said it felt better without. He was in love with her after the time he danced her. They danced, they went upstairs idk. How does it happen? How do you get started? I could have texted Serena and she def would have told me that night. But I knew I didn't want to find out from Serena. There was too much wrong with her. There was more wrong with her than there was with me.

My dad picked me up from school. I hate being picked up in a Lexus. And I know this is totally a first-world middle-class problem as Holly never tires of explaining. But it's like driving around in a marketing opportunity. I wish it was a Honda Civic or something. Like I would love if my dad's car was the same as Holly's. Holly's dad has a sheet of stainless steel under the driver's seat because the floor of the car rusted. It is a Toyota Corolla. He had an unfortunate experience with sea water. Once upon a time he was driving somewhere in bad weather and he did not notice that the road was underwater. He might have been stoned. I'm not saying Holly's dad is a stoner, but he's definitely not anti. He had to get the fire brigade to push him out. As a matter of fact the fire brigade was there anyway, marking the flooding and warning people not to drive into it. Holly's dad was not sure how he missed that because there were flashing lights. The car started straight away and he drove off. He forgot about it. But one day about a year later he sat into the car and the seat went straight through to the road. Luckily it didn't happen when he was moving, like if he went over a bump he would have been Dragging His Arse Along The Road At Sixty whatever. Holly's dad is just totally cool about all that. He got a friend to cut him a sheet of stainless. My dad would have taken the car sales company to court and he would have bought a new car. If something can be thrown away, my dad throws it.

So this is the conversation.

Me: I think Serena is getting bullied by some of the girls.

Dad: Really?

Me: Well like I don't know. Maybe. They were making comments about her today.

Dad: (Silence)

Me: (After a while) They were saying she's a slut but she's not. Like saying she goes with an older man.

Dad: Tsk tsk. Don't say words like that, Suzy. Serena is a nice girl.

Me: Harsh, Dad. I didn't say it, they did.

Dad: Well, it's not nice.

Me: Dad, I'm talking about the bitches. They're superbitches some of them. You should hear….

Dad: Suzy! That's enough. Don't say bitches. We have some rules in our house, you know.

Me: (Silence)

Dad: (Silence)

He drove slowly. It drove me crazy. He was a careful driver. He didn't even like to park his Lexus in town in case it got scratched. When he had to park it in town he sometimes put it in the disabled drivers' spaces because they're wider. If he does that I always ask to get out before he parks and I walk away. I will not be seen getting out of a Lexus with a non-disabled driver in a disabled driver parking space. I hate him when he does that. He just shrugs and says, The cripples get all the best spaces. Jesus fuck my life. I swear. He's like Mr Bean only SO not funny. His hand is shaking. I can see it. As soon as he lifts it off the wheel there's a tiny little shake like a frightened bird. In fact both of his hands are like birds. They've gotten small. Or else they were always small only I never noticed. His left hand shakes more than his right. And he's been biting his nails. He never bites his nails. It's like you never notice things about your dad until he has a heart attack.

So today he says, Suzy, you see that land out your window there? That's Castlemartin.

Me: I know, Dad.

Dad: And you probly know that a syndicate has put in a planning application for four hundred houses. Seemingly there's a housing shortage. He laughs. That's all me eye and Johnny Reilly of course. The auctioneers want it so the government gives it. A housing shortage is a matter of optics. And you probly know that Dan Kelleher is in that syndicate.

Me: Dad?

Dad: Well, they won't be getting any planning permission.

Me: Dad, what did you do? What did you do, Dad?

Dad: Never mind. But I'll tell you one thing for nothing: Kelleher is screwed.

Now I was scared. I don't know what my dad does. But he did other things before.

There was a sign by the side of the road that said No Trespassers. He pulled the car in beside it. There was a hole in the fence.

Stay there, he said to me.

He went through the hole in the fence as fast as a fox but the sleeve of his jacket caught in it. He worked it loose. About four cars went past while he was doing it. Then he walked out into the middle of the field. It took about a minute. It was a very big field. There were seven cows on the far side. They watched him. In the middle of the field he stopped. He had his back turned to me. I saw him doing something. And then I saw what he was doing. MY DAD WAS FUCKING PISSING IN A FIELD. Like we didn't have a toilet in our house. He stood the way men do, like slightly hunched but slightly leaning back. I could see it. It was a cold bright day and there was steam in the air in front of him. Then he did the flick flick thing and zipped up. Then he turned around. He looked happy idk I hardly ever see my dad happy. He was just grinning all over his face like a child. He got back out through the fence again and looked up and down the road. Then he got in.

What was that about, Dad?

I needed to go, he said.

And there was me thinking: That's a flood plain. When they build on that they'll make the river flooding worse. The houses on the edge will need to be built up. The service roads will flood. What kind of a fucking country do we live in idk.

Dad, whatever you did to Dan Kelleher, is it going to be trouble?

He'll never even know what hit him.

But the other guys in the syndicate thingy....

He shrugged. He pulled out onto the road and we moved on again.

At a snail's pace. A random car passed us out, blowing the horn. My dad gave them the finger. He was laughing. He looked at me and winked. Look at that fucking sign, he said, how did they get planning for that?

He was pointing to a new billboard that said, What think ye of Jesus? Whose son is he?

I don't know about the planning permission, but I think those signs are for weirdos and creepers. Like these guys actually imagine that real people think about things like that. Like I don't even know what it means. Like were Joseph and Mary his folks or was it God? Well, definitely Mary, everybody is agreed on that. But maybe it was the postman and the God thing is all my arse? Well, that's what I think anyway. If they had postmen. Or a passing centurion or one of those Good Samaritans you hear about. What about them? They can't all have been good.

My dad hit the steering wheel with the flat of his hand.

I pissed on the bastards, he said, I pissed on them.

So my brother crashed my mam's car and it was a total write-off. He got out and walked away. Not a scratch on him. My mam said he was lucky and a car was only a car. I saw her hug him so hard I thought she would stop his heart. My mam really loves my brother. I would have killed her there and then with a kitchen knife except for my brother Tony. I am crazy about him. I even know which knife I would use. It would be the one with a serrated edge on both sides.

They weren't worrying about the insurance. My mam was trying to work out how not to tell Dad. She would say she traded it in. She was getting a new one. I couldn't believe it. Of all the histories my family dreamt up, the one about my mam trading in her precious Audi was the crappiest. I knew my dad would not swallow it for a second. He would go ballistic.

And I was thinking, I almost lost my big brother. I was sad. Really sad. I felt like I was looking at a ghost. Like he was already dead and his body was in a field surrounded by broken bits of himself and my mam's Audi. And if nobody found him he would turn into a bundle of bones like Lucy and in a couple of million years some scientist would wonder if he was related to the high metal content in the soil. We studied Lucy when I was doing Biology. There was a bite mark on her pelvis. We had a good teacher then but she left. Someone buried Lucy three point two million years ago give or take and my guess is that she died the hard way and whoever buried her was broken-hearted. I have the feeling she was my age. I saw her bones on Wikipedia. It was sad.

And then my dad came home for his lunch and the freaking started. He already knew the whole story because one of his pals in the guards called him. My dad keeps the local guards sweet. He almost hit my brother. Then he almost hit my mam. They were screaming. It was Mam and my brother against my dad. And my mam screaming, Calm down, you'll have a fucking heart attack! All the usual stuff. And the price of the car. And the insurance wouldn't cover it. And my brother is a useless git. And the guards said there were no brake marks. I went to my room.

There were no brake marks on the road. I knew what was going on.

I know what a dysfunctional family is. I googled it. Fifteen signs you come from a dysfunctional family. Thirty-two ways you know you grew up in a dysfunctional family. What makes a functional family vs dysfunctional. Surviving dysfunctional families. I have twelve of the fifteen signs. I didn't even look at the thirty-two. I don't know, do people in families like mine ever actually kill each other? Like my dad could kill my brother. He hates him. I could kill my mam. My dad could kill my mam. Everything in our family is a secret until it's too late. My brother even tried to kill himself. That's what the no brake marks means. You see it on the news. The guards said there was No Evidence Of Braking at the scene. Suicide among young men is on the rise since The Crash. Nobody knows why. FFS. I hate my family. It Is The Worst. Every time. Every time I want to scream. I can feel something scream-ing inside me.

I took my brother's razor blades out of the drawer and sat on the bed. Like cutting yourself was meant to shut things out. I googled it. All you can think about is the pain. I took a blade out. I thought the first thing I should do is disinfect it. Like even skin has bacteria. I could still here the screaming. I heard my mam telling my dad to get the fuck out of her life. I undid my jeans and rolled them down. I pressed the blade against the soft part of my thigh, on the inside. I thought, Some day some guy is going to fall in love with me and when we're in bed he's going to look at my legs and say, what are these scars? Then someone would know what kind of a shit life I'm living right now. I pressed the blade but I couldn't make myself cut. I didn't have the guts. I put the blade back in the pack. I heard the door slamming downstairs and I heard my brother go to his room. The shouting was still happening. I went downstairs and called The Dog and we went out for a walk. Not to Regan's Glen. A normal day in my house.

Me and The Dog walking along the road. A car stopped and the window rolled down. It was the Bowles guy.

Hello, he said.

Hiya.

Need a lift?

Like, no?

Nice dog. What's his name?

The Dog.

Yes?

That's his name. The Dog. He belongs to my brother. If he was mine I'd call him Stupid.

The Bowles guy laughed.

That's a good one.

Thanks.

I just stopped to say you owe me for my recycling bin, you and your friend.

I blushed. I will never marry anybody because I Blush like literally All The Time. I go completely red. I looked into the car. The housekeeper was in there too. If I ever commit a crime I will confess everything the minute the cop says anything you say may be taken down and used against you in a court of law. Or whatever the Irish guards say. I just can't be arsed lying.

How did you know it was us?

We were watching you for ten minutes, weren't we, Grace?

We were sat there splitting our sides, Grace said.

Why didn't you stop us?

Too much fun. But when you broke the bloody window! We didn't know how to turn off the alarm. You got us into trouble. We don't want the police, do we, Grace?

Grace: Certainly not, Tom.

Tom: So, the thing is, you have to pay for the bin and the broken window.

Grace: And the call-out for the alarm.

Tom: Yeah, the call-out for the alarm. See, we didn't know how to reset it. We had to get a nice man to fix it.

He was a nice man, Grace said.

A big old grey-back crow pitched on the road in front of the car. There was something dead that I couldn't quite make out, a rabbit maybe. The crow looked like an old man throwing his weight around but not very sure of himself. Like a man ordering pints in a pub for people he didn't like. I was nervous. I'm never sure whether big people are joking or not. Like, I thought the Bowles guy was joking me. If he wasn't, I was in big trouble. I could get money for things from my dad and my mam but no way could I say I need to pay for the bin I set fire to up in Ballyshane.

I said, My dad hates you.

That changed his tune. He looked at Grace and Grace bent down so she could see out the window better.

Who is your dad, little girl? she said softly.

I shook my head. He wanted Ballyshane, but you got it. He thinks the house belongs to us.

Are you the local IRA or something? Grace said and the two of them laughed. They laughed like crazy. Then they drove away.

And we had Joe Daly in to fix something with the gutters. They were clogged or they were leaking idk there was damp on the wall and ceiling of my parent's bedroom and the en suite. And Joe said that there was work going on in Ballyshane, he was talking to one of the lads, and they were replacing some of the windows and they were putting in all timber-weighted sashes. They were getting them made in England. Proper conservation-grade stuff. It would be a beautiful job. And I could see my dad thinking he wouldn't have been able to afford to do that. Our windows were plastic Senator windows but when I looked out I didn't hear classical music like in the ad. I just heard nothing. Like we live in the country. Nothing really happens most of the time. And anyway, they're double-glazed and argon gas.

Joe Daly always talks to me like I'm out clubbing every night.

Who's the latest lucky man, Suzy?

There's no lucky man.

I hear you were in Qubin's on Saturday night. Great craic in Qubin's.

I was never in Qubin's, Joe.

Hoho now, that's not what I hear. Sure the lads are flocking after you, girl. That's what I hear anyway. And why wouldn't they?

I wanted to find a rusty knife and gut him slowly.

My fucking life. I swear.

What happened was my brother was out with friends. It is one of life's mysteries how he passes exams, he totally prefers the pub. And someone said, Here's to poor old Nigger. And my brother left. It was a pub somewhere in Darkest Ireland, not near his uni. Probably Keniry's because that's where they drink. It's like an old man's pub. And a couple of the boys went after him because they knew. But he was running and they didn't realise at first. They thought he just went outside. When they saw him running through the car park they started to run too. He got to the car. They didn't get there in time. He drove away. They told me he had hash but there might have been something else too. They always had hash. That was about nine and the accident happened at four a.m. Where did the lost hours go? The boys didn't know. Tosser Kennedy said to me: We're worried about him, Suzy, like it was bad enough with Nigger, but your bro? I asked him what he meant. He said my brother was depressed. I didn't say he'd be the odd one out in our family if he wasn't.

They told me this on the Saturday after the accident, they came over to my house to play Minecraft with my brother and while they were waiting for him they told me the whole story. Engineers love Minecraft, in my humble opinion they are the most boring in the world, worse than medicine. So my brother left the pub about nine and at four a.m. he drove through a fence on a bend in the road and fell down into a field and the car rolled over twice and when it stopped he got out and walked home and went to bed. What did he do in the meantime and where did he go? Someone said they thought he spent a couple of hours driving around, diffing and doing donuts. It's possible. My brother is a maniac. But I don't think it's what he did. Like I should ask him, but we don't talk a lot. Nobody in my family talks. We are secret agents.

So I asked Tosser. He said he already asked him: Like, where did you go, Tony? And my brother goes, None of your fucking business, Tosser.

And that was that.

Subtle, I said, you really applied psychology to that one.

He laughed, Guess why they call me Tosser?

Tosser is all right but he's a certified knobhead. Once he used to have a rear-wheel drive Beamer and he used to go diffing and stuff. When we'd see a set of donuts somewhere on the road my brother would say, Tosser was on the rantan last night. Everybody said Tosser was a knobhead and would end up dead, but he just grew

116

out of it. He was one hundred per cent langer until he was about eighteen. My mam used to hate him but now she is all right about him. But Tosser is actually a softie, I don't know what kind of an engineer he'll make. Like you're supposed to be all logic and calculation and hard. He is into the environment too. I said, You're in the wrong business, Tosser, you're going to spend your life destroying environments! He thought that was hilarious.

I guess I'm sort of a mascot for my brother's friends. It's hard to get taken seriously.

And then I found out that my mam wanted my brother to get counselling and my dad said that was just shit and counselling was a waste of money, counsellors were all nuts themselves, that's how they get into it, they should be called coinsellers because they were coining it, he should get into the business himself. And my mam said she was worried and the accident didn't sound right, like what was he doing on that road anyway? And my dad said he needed a kick up the arse and he had half a mind to give it to him. I could hear them arguing in the kitchen when I was in the downstairs toilet. I wanted to hit my head off the sink. I even put my hands over my ears, but I needed to get dressed up again.

When my grandad died there was a dispute about where he was to be buried. He was supposed to be buried in the same grave as my granny, who I never met. Her side of the family owned graves. My dad said no way was he burying Grandad there unless he had control of the grave. Like you have title deeds to a grave. They said no. My dad said the grave was shit, they needed a new stone, the old stone was full and it was basically a crap stone and no way was he burying his dad in someone else's grave. They said no. My dad always gets his way. So there only was like three days. That's how long they keep a dead body for. There's church stuff et cetera. So my dad bought a new grave and got it dug up. They say open and close a grave, like it's a door. He told my mam it was just a move in the negotiations. Like he had this six-foot hole in the graveyard waiting for my grandad and it was a move? They said he was going against his own mother's dying wish, and his father's dying wish and nearly everybody's dying wish. So the morning of the funeral came and there was this big standoff in our kitchen. Their side and our side. I thought the kitchen was a bad place for it because of The Availability Of Knives. In the end he won. He already had the deed of conveyance, all they had to do was Sign On The Line. So my dad added to his property portfolio and my grandad got buried with his one true love. And her side of the family never talked to us again.

My mam came up and told me to stop moping in my room.

You spend your life in here, she said. Get out and get some fresh air. Fresh air is good for you.

Like my mam never goes outside unless it is to get into her car. Even when she exercises, which starts every January and ends in March, she goes to the gym. The gym is in a hotel and she drives into the underground car park and takes the lift. I don't think she ever breathes un-air-conditioned air except at home, like office (aircon) => car (aircon) => lift (aircon) => gym (aircon). Like I googled it and there was a study which showed that the air in gyms contains unacceptable levels of dust, formaldehyde and CO2 and the levels were higher than most legal standards of air quality indoors. I'm waiting for my mam to get a respiratory disease which is linked to formaldehyde. I googled that too. She would be the fittest person in the world to die because she couldn't breathe. Of natural causes anyway.

Her company had a cyber attack. She said someone was trying to steal their intellectual property. Like, Hello, Mam, what's intellectual about property? They were freaking about it and her job was to calm them down.

I texted Serena and told her about the Bowles guy stopping. I said we were in trouble. Serena texted back: b4 I tell u anything u need to promes not to tell a sole ☺.

Serena is shit at English and even shitter at text. I texted back: WTF are u talking about?

She replied, SHOUTY CAPS MUCH.

I just sent her a smiley face.

The phone rang immediately. It was her.

Serena: I know where your brother was.

Me: I don't want to know.

Serena: (Silence).

Me: Is that what you called me for?

Serena: (obviously pissed at me) I thought you wanted to know?

Me: Like if you're calling to tell me it must be bad news.

Serena: And I have a contact on alt.com. He's twenty-five and he's into the same kinks as me exactly and he's really good-looking he sent me his pic and we're going to meet up when he comes down which he does because he's a salesman.

Me: Jesus wept. Have you nothing at all between your ears?

Serena: He goes up to Ballyshane.

Me: The fucking salesman?

Serena: Tony.

Me: How do you know?

Serena: So now you want to know?

Me: Fuck off, Serena.

I hung up. I went into my brother's room. He wasn't there. I opened all his drawers and looked through them. I lifted the mattress on his bed. I checked the pockets of his jackets and coats in the wardrobe. I even checked his shoes. What was I looking for? I don't know. But if he had a secret life, like if he was up in Ballyshane the night of the accident, there must be something. In the end all I found was a packet of Rizlas and a packet of Durex, not Tingle Me idk just common or garden condoms. I already knew he smoked dope. They all did. And everybody says a packet of Durex is a Reasonable Precaution Against Life. They told me nothing.

We're living in this dead inside where nothing moves except us. Our selves are the only thing we can hurt. I started cutting that evening. I did it in the shower. I almost didn't do it. Then I fucking slashed it. A deep slash, no thinking. Just above my T-shirt line, on my left arm. Who was I slashing? Me. There was so much blood. I think I went too deep. I thought if I pushed my finger into it I would feel my own bone, my skeleton inside my own body, the Lucy in me. I saw the blood wash out pale and pink, down my arm, down my legs, spinning down the plughole. I thought: I could fucking do myself, I could do it just now. And then I sat down and cried. The water came down on my head and burned away tears and blood. It fell on me like fire. It was the pain. The pain was me.

I did not want to be me.

I covered it with Elastoplast but it leaked. I panicked and put two more Elastoplasts on it. I tried to pull the edges together with the sticking plaster. I remembered reading somewhere that you could do it with Superglue, but I didn't think we had any. It was eleven thirty at night. What if I bled to death in my sleep? I googled deep wounds but I couldn't look at that stuff. I thought, If I die at least they'll know they fucked me up big time. I thought about writing a suicide note. But, like what if I didn't die, I would feel so stupid tomorrow. And my mam would kill me. Then the blood stopped leaking and I had time to think about the pain. Note to self: Never do this again. Like I actually wrote that on my phone and saved it as a reminder. It was so sore. At least I wouldn't end up going to Accident and Emergency. That's where they took my brother. He had to have his head X-rayed. I bet a million they found it was completely empty. Not worth the X-ray. No brain, no brain damage. They let him out as fast as they took him in. My dad collected him. Sometimes babies are born without a brain – I remember that from my baby phase. Anencephaly. The condition of having all or part of the cerebral hemispheres absent. There was a boy who lived to be twelve. He just never had a thought.

The pain kept me awake and so I heard my brother coming home at two in the morning. Tosser Kennedy was the Designated Driver. I watched them. Tosser and my brother sat in the car for five minutes, then my brother got out. He was seriously drunk. Like when he got out of the car he tried to lean on the door to say something to Tosser and he missed the door and fell face first back in. Then he got out by going on his knees. This is how I see it: my brother is falling into a deep well, when he will reach the bottom nobody knows. Some evening I will come home from school and my mam will be watching the *Bake Off* and she'll say, Your brother is dead. Then she'll flick the channels.

OK, that's not possible. She would be Freaking, she wouldn't just be sitting there. And my dad would stay in the office until very late so he wouldn't have to deal with it. And someone would blame me. But really it's all of us, my brother included.

And how would he die? He would drive my mam's next car through a stone wall, or jump in the river like John Brown, or maybe he would cut his throat with a razor blade. Or maybe, like me, he would just choke to death in the dead air of our family. Something would happen and he would be dead. I already had a broken heart.

It was snowing. We call it snow in Ireland but, as Serena Never Tires Of Telling Me, they have different varieties of snow of which ours is the pissiest. She Has Seen The Real Thing. It was a thin straight snow and when it landed on the ground it was the size and shape of a grain of rice. But minute by minute it was covering the ground and the ground was frozen. Like the earth would break if you hit it with a hammer, the whole world would crack down the middle. Frozen things break. Standing at the bus stop with Holly. I love Holly like the best thing you can love, we don't even need to talk to understand each other. We were so cold. We stamped around and tried to rub each other warm. The bus was probably delayed by the snow. In Canada and places they have snowploughs but in Ireland if two snowflakes fall it's a weather alert code red. I love the weather forecast. It's my favourite programme. Holly nudged me and started to sing 'My Resistance is Low'. And I sang along. It was funny because Holly had a cold. We were happy. My phone rang. It was Serena. She was crying. Like Serena has a liquidity problem. She breaks down under stress, even if it's only stress she imagined.

I couldn't understand what she was saying.

Slow down, girl, I said, what are you telling me, I can't hear properly.

Holly came close and put her ear to the phone. We looked at each other.

Holly said, She's saying she's in the hospital.

I tried to talk. Serena, Serena, slow down. Serena. Are you in hospital?

I couldn't get her to stop. Then the call ended. Did she end it? Or was it my crappy signal?

Holly said, We better go see her. Do you think she...?

What? Do I think she what?

She sounded shook. Like really shook.

Well, she's sick.

She said something about an ambulance, Holly said.

I could see what Holly was saying. I said: The night we set fire to the bin I helped her undress...

Holly gave me the retina scan look. Like she was thinking, Bitch, you did Serena too!

No way, I said, don't you start. She was frozen and she couldn't get out of her clothes. I helped her that's all.

And your point is?

My point is she cuts. I saw her legs. The other times she got dressed in the bathroom and came out in her dino onesie. But this time I saw her legs. She cuts and she cuts bad.

Holly walked away to the other side of the bus stop, clapping her hands and stamping her feet. She waited over there for like thirty seconds, looking at the advertising, which was for *Fifty Shades of Grey*. Like we saw the trailer on YouTube and it looks like it's about tall buildings, big offices and helicopters. Holly said it looked like it was about a bank. We didn't read the book yet. I watched Holly watching the ad and when she came back I saw she had been crying. Her face was wet under her eyes. She put her hand on my arm and squeezed hard. I pulled away. I knew what she was telling me. She must have seen something.

Fuck off, I said, none of your business.

Does it hurt?

I nodded. All the time. That's why I did it.

The bus came just then. We got on. Some boys from the boys' school hooted and whistled. They always do. Boys take a lot longer to grow up. Down in the middle of them was Jason Clancy who fancies Holly. He used to be with Helen Minihan but she dumped him. She is a bitch. She is with a guy who has a job in the hotel now. Jason Clancy has a car. He smokes which is ew. He fancies getting into her pants anyway. I bet his hands smell of smoke. I don't think it's a soulmate thing. Holly ignores him. We sat second row from the front, that way we could just look at the road. There was an old woman with shopping bags in the front seat. She talked to herself and answered back. She was talking about something that happened at the shop. The neck of her, the brazen neck, I'm shopping here twenty years, miss. I have to call the manager. Go on then and we'll see what he has to say about it and I coming in here this past twenty years, I know my rights.

All the time Holly and I said nothing. We didn't look at each other. We got off at the hospital stop. The snow was in little hard bits. People wore long coats and hats and scarves and gloves. I was shaking because the hospital terrifies me. I get nightmares about my dad's operation. I see them opening his chest like a box. Inside that box there are monsters. Like things out of *Alien*. Like when they put the guy on the table with all the food and he's twisting around and then the thingy comes out of his chest. Like the lizard thing. Idk. And Sigourney Weaver omg. It comes out of her tummy. Like giving birth to an alien lizard character. I had that dream one night. The guy who made the alien also made the aliens for *Close Encounters of the Third Kind*. What are the other two kinds? And what if there's more than three? I blame Serena for all that shit.

She was in Ward 2B. They told us at the reception. They don't care why a patient is in. That's someone else's problem. They look at their computer screen and a ward number comes up and that's that. I suppose if they knew why every person in the hospital was there they would die of the weight of all the pain. She's in 2B, next please? We went up there but the nurse told us she was asleep. I was a bit relieved. I didn't want to find out what happened. I think Holly was relieved too. We were just about to go away when the nurse stopped us.

If you wait for a bit we'll have to wake her up to do her stats.

Oh OK.

Are you friends of hers?

We nodded.

She's very upset about something. Any ideas, girls?

We shook our heads. I could have told her Serena is Very Upset about things often, it's a thing she does. But it felt like I would be letting her down. And then, we all get upset. Except maybe Holly. We're all just moving from one crisis to the next like the rest of the country. Like we're supposed to be in recovery but everyone older than my brother is emigrating and the only way to see a doctor is to overdose on mood modifiers.

My phone rang. It was my brother. He asked me where I was. He said Mam was looking for me. There was some kind of protest outside my dad's office and she was hoping I wasn't there. I said I was visiting a friend in hospital, and what was the protest about? My brother said: One of Dad's evictions looks like it went wrong. Talk to you later. And he hung up.

Like Dad's evictions usually go well as long as you're Dad.

The smell of hospitals. Farts and urine and disinfectant and stale clothes and something that might be blood. And the sound of machines. Who knows what the machines are for? And I always have the feeling that under the whole thing there are dead people. Like, where do they put the corpses? It has to be in the cellar or basement. I don't like being near dead people unless I know them personally and even then I'd prefer them to be alive. And where do they put the people with infectious diseases? What if there is an Ebola patient only they don't know it's Ebola yet? The first signs are the same as the flu.

Oh she's waking up now, the nurse said. She pointed at the big window in front of her desk. You can go in if you like.

Serena was as pale as ash. Her eyes had red rims around them. Her hair was stuck to her head. When she looked at me I couldn't bear to look her back.

Hi, guys, she said. She did not smile.

I sat at one side of the bed and Holly sat at the other. We didn't know what to say. After a bit I saw Holly take Serena's hand. Serena let her. They held hands all the time after that except when they took her blood pressure. Eventually I said, Leary nearly had a heart attack today.

Holly said, You're lucky he's not in the next bed. You'd get the Weimar Republic all over again.

Leary was big on the Weimar Republic. There was a question on every test. Origins and growth of the fascist regimes in Europe; the Nazi state in peace and war. He thinks the Nazis are coming again.

I said: There was a rat got into the photocopy room and he needed to do like thirty copies of thirty pages or something, you know the way, like he's Mr Handout, and everybody knows he's terrified of small animals. Remember that weird sort of diary to camera item he did once? Girls, we all have our hangups. I'd say the rat was terrified too. Locked up with Leary. Everybody's nightmare. It was probably a girl rat.

Holly said, You could have had Leary and the rat in here.

That got a half-smile from Serena. She squeezed Holly's hand. A nurse came and did the things they do, temperature, blood pressure, pulse. It's weird. They put a clothes peg on your finger and a pump-up sleeve on your arm and they swipe something across your forehead and touch your ear. It's like the Last Rites or something religious. Everything OK, pet? Yes, nurse. Be sure and call if you need anything. Yes, nurse. All your signs are fine anyway.

They are so calm. She went out again pushing her clinky trolley. A little smile from Serena. Like she knows that no one sees the signs. Serena is superior, she knows it somehow, she just assumes it, I would say it is her biggest fault. It's one of the things that makes me hate her. When I hate her. It makes me want to hurt her.

I said: How did you do it?

She looked away. Holly almost lost her hand but held on to it in time.

Serena, I said, the night of the bin fire, I saw your legs. I saw the cuts.

She turned to me. Her eyes were hot and dry.

Some friend you are.

We need to talk about it.

Fuck you, Serena said.

Holly looked at me. I knew she was thinking, Look who's talking! So I took my jacket off. Then I took my school jumper off. Then I unbuttoned my left sleeve and rolled it up. It would not go up far enough so I pushed it the rest of the way. Serena stared at my arm. Holly started to cry. The tight sleeve made the cuts look red and fat. They looked like rips in a mattress with the stuffing showing.

I said, We have to fucking talk about it. Right?

Outside Serena's window the snow was thickening. I thought you could almost follow a single flake from the sky to the ground. But your eye could not distinguish the white from the white. All you could know was the falling. We are three girls on a see-saw, three of us on one side, but the mass on the other side is so much. We are so high up we will never come down. So high we can hardly breathe. See-saw, Margery Daw, sold her bed and lay on straw.

And later Holly and I were like zombies. We walked back out to the bus stop. We stood at the bus stop. The snow was a fine sugar sprinkled over everything. We didn't talk. We didn't look at each other. Then the bus came. It was crowded and we had to stand. We got off at our stop and went our own ways. The only thing that was said between us was coming down in the lift at the hospital. Holly goes: Why didn't you tell me? And I said: Because I'm afraid. She said: Afraid of me? And I'm like:

No, I'm afraid of what's happening to me. And she had no answer to that because now she was afraid too. Holly had an answer to everything when we were small.

So it turns out she overdosed on Xanax. It is not an easy thing to overdose on. You need a stockpile. It took her an hour and a half to swallow them. She took them with vodka. Vodka is the go-to liquor for teen suicides. I googled Xanax. It won't kill you except it'll stop your breathing. Like it's hard to be alive and not breathing. But the vodka nearly killed her. Her mother was calling her for dinner and when she didn't answer she came up to her room. She saw the blister-packs and she saw Serena. She saw that she wasn't moving, there was vomit on her bed and on the floor, a bad smell. She called the ambulance. In the ambulance her breathing stopped. They got it going again somehow. Ambulance people are ace. She didn't know much about what happened, they told her things. Her dad works in the hospital but he didn't come down once to see her.

My first idea was that she met Mr alt.com and that he did something bad, like bad idk maybe raped or worse. What's worse than rape? But she didn't meet him. So she said anyway. She said she was getting her head together. Quick WhatsApp summary:

In case ur overthinking I did not meet the guy.

That's good news anyway.

Thanks.

Welcome.

Ur so jugmental.

I just want you to get well.

Im getting my head together ill be different just watch.

Cool baby love you.

!!???

That was her last message: !!???

So now she has compulsory counselling and a psychiatrist. Her dad is pissed about it. It's not good for his reputation. And her mother is concerned. That's what she told my mother. My mother said to me, If you ever do something like that I'll kill you. Which is ironic really. Suicide by matricide. Or would it be infanticide? I'm scared that Serena will tell her psychiatrist about my cuts and he'll call my doctor or something, whatever they do. Official channels. Or maybe he'd phone my mam. I stopped cutting for a week while Serena was inside. Then I extended it by a week. It felt good to be clean, but I wanted to go back to it real bad. I am a recovering self-harmer. I think. Idk. I googled Alcoholics Anonymous, the Twelve Steps, but it's all about God and I don't do God. Like, We sought through prayer and meditation to improve our conscious contact with God. Like prayer and meditation ffs. Conscious contact with God, Jesus wept. Like ever heard of Twitter? Twitter is the Antichrist of meditation and if you're not there you're not anywhere. God does not tweet. Like: Thou shalt not kill @ISRAELITES @EVERYBODYELSE.

But then my brother broke three plates on the floor. He did it like a woman in a movie, even stamped his feet. I saw them break, all the little needle points, the blades, the shards. When a plate breaks it leaves little needles of pottery everywhere. If I walked on them in bare feet they would lacerate my soles. It would be like walking on hot coals. It happened because my dad would not give him the keys of his car. Something terrible was behind it idk maybe drugs. And my brother said my dad was a knobhead. And my mother slapped him across the face and I could see he was going to slap her back, but he didn't. And my dad left the room and my mam said to go easy on him because the protests were getting to my dad, like every loonie lefty in the country was out trying to keep non-compliant tenants in their houses. Non-compliant tenant is my dad's code for poor. And of course they were all commies. And my dad was trying to get a court order to stop them. And my brother Tony said it served him right. And my mam almost hit him again. It was idk seriously painful. My dad and mam epic fail the stress test every time. So much for parenting skills.

And that evening I started on my thighs.

Because you can shut things out.

You can drown noise.

You can bury anything under your skin. Drown things under the skin.

A scar becomes a scab and fades away.

So I stayed a night with Serena in her house. Her mother thought it might help because Serena talks to me. And I would do anything not to be at home. We had a tidy little dinner with her parents. They didn't talk. I had the impression they were against talking during eating. Maybe there is a medical theory about that, the digestion idk. And Serena did the pollock smile all the way through. Miss Goody Two Shoes. I wanted to gut her with the breadknife and saw her into manageable parts and distribute them evenly over the entire county. For the fucking crows. And they had DVDs for us to watch afterwards. Her father was on call and about ten he was called out to an emergency at the hospital. They have eye emergencies apparently. Maybe accidents idk. Her mother said goodnight and to turn out the lights, Daddy could be all night. And we turned out the lights. And we undressed together. And we saw each others' cuts. And we talked it over. For me it was the noise. For her it was the silence. Same difference. Nobody tells us anything. She touched my cuts and I touched hers. Like Doubting Thomas in the Bible. I put my hand into her wound. Except I never doubted. We didn't talk much idk. By midnight it was over. It was the first good sleep I had in weeks. We decided we needed to run away.

So Serena is religious. Her whole family is. Her father goes to meetings and he serves Communion at Mass on the Sundays when he's not on duty. He's a member of some secret religious group, like Opus Dei or something idk a tight little male group of pious wankers. Even Serena didn't know the name. Her father's hands were blessed by the Pope. I wouldn't care who blessed his hands if he was operating on me, I'd rather have someone else. He is like totally creepy, you have no idea. He wears these silent shoes. When he comes into a room if you're not looking you don't know. Like when my dad comes upstairs you can hear him starting in the hall before he even puts one foot on a step, but Serena's dad could be opening the bedroom door and you wouldn't hear. Serena says she never heard her dad and mam fight, not once, not even raised voices. Her mam never disagreed with her father while she was there. In fact, she said, they never discussed anything. I told her about the terrible rows my parents had. I said someday someone is going to kill my mam. She said she'd do it for me and for a bit we used to pretend that we were planning it and we'd keep coming up with brilliant ideas. Like one idea was that we'd electrocute her in the shower. And another time we thought what if we fed her to the pigs. It was something we saw in a film. But we didn't know anybody with pigs. Well, Holly's dad kept pigs but only two and we didn't think two would be enough to eat a whole human being. Serena said she could get one of the boys to fix the brakes on her car, but that would involve a boy and we couldn't trust them. And I didn't want to ask what Serena would do to the boy to get him to do it. I thought it was a bad plan. Our whole problem was that we couldn't work out how to get away with it and we decided in the end that people who really kill other people aren't worried about getting away because being in prison isn't as bad as living with them. And I wasn't there yet.

Holly's mam and dad go on marches. Sometimes Holly goes too. Once she WhatsApped me a pic of herself with some famous political guy. Her dad makes jokes like: Why do socialists drink herbal tea? Because proper tea is theft. I don't get it. Even when Holly explains it to me I don't get it. It is not like me to miss a joke. I say Mam and Holly says Mammy. But she wouldn't kill either of her parents. It's like the model of a normal family only weird. Like keeping pigs. Growing potatoes. Keeping bees. Sometimes her mam picks her up from school on the first day of her period. It's weird idk maybe it's what you do if you're an anarchist. They are leftover hippies. But tbh I like them. Her dad lives in a ratty cardigan and a parka jacket. He smells nice. My dad smells of Brut and Right Guard, so many ways to fill your armpits with great-smelling, odour-fighting, high-fiving, rim-hanging, trash-talking, ball-spiking, pointing-to-the-crowd confidence and protection.

I googled it.

I know. I'm the superbitch googler. I'm OCD tbh. I'm like addicted to Google. I've even contributed to Google Translate. For Irish. I have Google set to Gaeilge. The ten things we know to be true. #1 Focus on the user and all else will follow. Google is my past, my wider resource community, my answer to everything. Except you never get actual answers. Should I have lesbian sex with my best friend? Answers: Should I have called in sick to have lesbian sex with my best friend? Me and my friend had the most amazing sex ever. It happened to me: I'm a lesbian pillow princess. The thirty-four signs you are actually dating your best friend. I have nine of them. FFS. Great just isn't good enough.

Serena's father's name is William and Holly told us that he came round their house one time to hand out leaflets with pictures of dead foetuses and her father christened him Willy The Right To Life. Her father said he was an asshole and a bullshit surgeon and he spent more time on his knees than he did operating. I don't know if any of that is true. But I knew that if ever Serena's father found out about her fucking boys, with or without condoms, and so far it was all without, or so she said, he would either kill her or throw her out whichever came first. My mother isn't religious but she voted against abortion. She subscribed to The

Floodgates Theory, which is basically if we do anything about anything the arse would fall out of everything else including shit we hold dear. My dad didn't vote. I don't think my brother was old enough to vote at the time but he would have voted the same way as my mam because that's what he's like. People know how you've voted, even though it's a secret ballot. They can say, Oh that house votes for so and so. I don't know how that gets out, it's like some secret system. When Serena's father met my mam after the referendum he said, We won. My mother just looked at him. She thinks doctors are gods but she doesn't like him. You don't have to like gods.

I asked Serena once about the sex thing and her father and what he would say if he found out. She said he would kill her. She said he never did anything wrong. She didn't even know how she was conceived. She couldn't possibly imagine her father Having Actual Sex, knowing what she knew about it. It must have been the fucking Immaculate Conception then, I said. Like, I said, everybody knows enough to know that. She just laughed like there was a big secret. There are not as many secrets as people think and the ones that are real are important. You can see sex on the net any day. It's just what does it feel like? No way all the ooohing and aaahhhing that goes on is for real. Like they're not even good actors. They're crap actors as a matter of fact. It's well known. Otherwise famous people like Brad Pitt or Cillian Murphy would be doing porn on their days off. Everybody loves Cillian Murphy's eyes. He would be the superbitch pornstar of all pornstars.

So my theory is Serena wants to get pregnant. It's not something she knows about, it's like a Deep and Secret Desire that even she hasn't been allowed to know. Somewhere deep down she wants to be found out by her father. That's why she keeps doing it without any protection. This will be some kind of revenge on Willy The Right To Life. On the other side, there's Sigmund Freud the world-famous psychologist who would probably say that she wants to get pregnant by her father idk. He had some weird theories. But you can buy condoms in all sorts of places, which was not an option available to Freud, and Serena has plenty of money. Like neither of us needs to ask for it. We have actual bank accounts. Holly has a Post Office account with her savings in it. Serena says savings are so last century. She can't wait to get a credit card. She keeps asking her father for one. And she has this like slight American twangy thingy idk it's like the way her voice rises a bit into the nose. It's hard to describe, and when you listen for it it's not there, but you feel it. And sometimes she can do that American kitty thing, being all pouty and cutie pie. I've seen her playing that game with her father and he loves it. The pet daughter. I googled alpha male and it turns out the alpha males respond to that kind of thing. I don't know about beta males or the others. History does not record. But Serena knew it from the start. She was born to it. And it makes me sick. Like Projectile Vomiting Sick.

And I look at them, her pouting at him, and I wonder what the scene will be when she says, Dad, I have some good news, there will be a new little Willy The Right in nine months time. Or seven or whatever.

It will not be pretty.

And now it's all about an abortion referendum. Willy The Right To Life is all psyched up about it. They're going to close the floodgates. Willy and his gang don't give a Flying Fuck what happens once the baby pops as long as he's baptised and Saved For God. I baptise you in the Name of the F and the S and the HG, Right, Fuck Off. This time the referendum seems to be about overturning the last one idk or maybe it's about not having a referendum. You mostly only hear Willy's side and for them it's always the last battle. Holy people willying all over the TV or the radio. Or maybe it's about gays idk. Or maybe that WAS the last one. In this country we keep doing referendums until they turn out right. Ireland is the superbitch referendum location. Is this the way it always is? History does not.

And thus Serena's father is doing his willying thing on the radio, this time it's about some poor woman who died. They got him into the studio to talk about foetal abnormality, which I know all about from my baby phase. They got him on so he could say that abortion was the wrong way to treat foetal abnormality and that even abnormal babies have a right to life, better one minute of life than none at all, mothers are selfish if they want to terminate a viable baby and all that crap. Like I want to say what about the babies that don't have a brain? What about the one that lived twelve years and never had a thought in all that time? What about that baby's parents? I never want to have a baby. It's just too much idk it's not fair.

So this is what's happening: Serena and me and Holly are on the bus and the driver has the radio playing and it's Wednesday half day so we're listening to the news and there's Serena's father saying all this shit. And I say, To listen to him you'd think he loves children. And Serena starts to cry. And then I'm crying and that starts Holly off. The three of us, just sitting in the bus, waiting for our stop, crying our eyes out because Serena's father is Willy The Right To Life and he doesn't love Serena. And I try to say I'm sorry but I can't.

So it turns out my dad is in trouble with the Revenue. They went through his books and they Invited Him In For A Conversation ^—^, and the subject of the conversation was how he owed them a couple of million euros. It turned out his business plan was really brilliant: Don't Pay Tax. He should get Entrepreneur Of The Year.

And my mam had to go too because she was a director in the company. And she couldn't believe what was happening because he didn't tell her beforehand. At least that's what she kept saying when they got home. I can't believe this is happening. And my dad was just like, Whatever. He kept saying they weren't going to get him and my mother kept saying you can't beat the Revenue and he said, If you owe them two euro you can't beat them, but if you owe them two million you hold all the cards. My mam just went like LOL. Like I think that was something he read somewhere. No way would my dad come up with something as stupid as that on his own. The Revenue is like The Great Satan to my mam, resistance is futile, so she was saying they should sell the houses and pay the debt. But my dad was saying no way, they bought most of them during The Boom and they were in negative equity since The Crash, they wouldn't even clear their mortgages, did she want them to end up owing the tax to the banks instead of the government? The Crash didn't hurt my dad very bad because when people can't afford to buy houses they have to rent them, and people sell their houses cheap and my dad buys them. It was a win-win situation for him, or so he said. But now it turns out he wasn't paying any tax. Maybe that wasn't such a big win. And my mother was talking about leaving him unless he sorted it out and he was saying, Take it easy, there's always a way.

I swear I would die if they split up. Never mind the murder business. I know there is something wrong with me ffs.

And then my dad says, like out of the blue, totally unconnected: That fucker Bowles up at Ballyshane, he joined the fucking golf club.

Like it was the end of the world.

As far as my dad was concerned this represented a massive betrayal on the part of the committee who tbh didn't even know my dad hated him and wouldn't give a shit anyway, money is money and golf clubs are all about money. Like I would have thought Bowles was too short for a golf club, but maybe they have mini ones. Like toy-size sticks. And my dad wouldn't be able to play up there any more. Even though he only plays there when he is Doing A Deal. My dad is the most unfit man I ever met. He gets heavy breathing on the stairs. And it's not because Mam is upstairs waiting for him. Holly says he is a Cartoon Capitalist Fatcat. Less like a cat there is no one in Ireland. My dad is more of a Cartoon Capitalist Slug frankly.

Mam: The Revenue will cancel your sub fast enough.

Dad: That was below the belt.

Mam: You haven't a clue, have you?

Dad: We'll all have to take a bit of pain, but everything will be all right in the end. We'll tighten our belts a bit and tough it out. We're the squeezed middle. They need us.

Mam: If you tighten your belt you'll bust a gut. You're the squeezed middle all right.

I could see my dad's hand shaking again. And he kept pinching his left arm. I googled it. It didn't come up but I got fifty-four point nine million hits about heart attacks. It seems if you google left arm everything that turns up involves a coronary. But what shocked me most was that he looked afraid. And a bit panicked. Even though everything he was saying was cool it, don't lose the rag, I think he was frightened. I wanted my mam to see it too but.

But my mam doesn't really look at my dad any more. Like maybe she never did idk but she doesn't now. I don't know if she doesn't want to see him or she can't see him or just to her he's not there. But every time I see her not seeing him it hurts me. She looks at me all right. She hates me.

And there was no dinner that night. I made toast and two boiled eggs and I took them up to my room and no one said anything. Like normally it's, No Eating In Your Room, Suzy. God is against eating in your room. The government is against it. Rules are rules. It Is A Crime Equal To Mass Murder. But I got to eat my toast and two boiled eggs sitting on my bed texting Serena and Holly on WhatsApp with my earphones in and my music on. I could hear someone diffing out at Ballyshane cross. I probably knew who it was too tbh. There would be donuts on the road. My mam gets nervous when she sees the tyre tracks. She thinks some guy is going to come round the corner spinning his wheels and crash into her sideways and Everybody Will Die. But differs never killed anybody, at least not while they were diffing. Maybe before or afterwards. They drive too fast and mostly the cars are shite. Serena and Holly were talking about the murder on our group WhatsApp convo. Serena heard that the guards were following a definite lead. It was on the news. They were trying to guess who did it. It had to be someone we knew, because on the telly it always is. In fact it should be the husband.

Only she was single.

And Serena WhatsApped me that she had a totally dreamy guy on alt.com and he had exactly the same kinks as her.

WhatsApp Me: dont tell me any more i dont want to know

WhatsApp Serena: were totally into it

She sent me a screen shot of their convo. It went:

Larrydemaster: babe you r legend thanks for the pics

Serena: r u into kinks? BDSM?

Larrydemaster: Totes babe. Bondage rape humiliation public.

Serena: I ♥ you

WhatsApp Me: You told a complete fucking stranger that you're into BDSM? jesus wept.

WhatsApp Serena: We sole mates

And I could still hear them shouting downstairs even through the earphones and the WhatsApp sounds and the diffing and the music. And some time around eleven I heard a bang and then there was silence for a while. I took my earphones out. Then I heard the front door closing and my dad's car starting and driving away. And then I heard my mam crying. And then my brother came in and I heard my mother screaming. So I went downstairs and my brother had blood all over his face and maybe something wrong with his nose and he was coughing a lot.

What else is going to happen in our family?

My mam is like: Where were you until now, Tony?

Nevermind where I was.

How did this happen to you?

I had something bad to eat. I'm going to bed. I need to lie down.

My dad never came home that night. Maybe he went to Miss Morocco and she took pity on him and let him make that shitty tea crap. And maybe he spent the night changing nappies and bottle-feeding the baby idk. My dad was never into babies. Like once my mam's sister changed a nappy in front of him and he went pale. They don't change nappies at the Golf Club.

But he didn't come back. And in the morning when I came downstairs my mam was like repeat dialling his mobile and she was still crying. And tbh I always thought it was my mam who would walk out because that's the way she is. I never thought my dad would leave. But it looked like he left us and switched off his mobile phone. Which is like the decree nisi of the internet age. I read about decree nisi when I googled divorce. We don't do decree nisi in Ireland.

She looked at me and she said, He has to turn it on when he goes to the office.

And I said, That's like two hours' time, Mam.

And she said, I know.

Where's Tony? I said.

Upstairs in bed.

Didn't he go to the hospital?

He can't. He was in a fight and if he goes in they'll report him.

I stared at her. I was thinking, What if he has a brain injury?

I said, Seriously, Mam, he might be hurt.

But she just kept dialling. She has a Huawei. It's a crap phone but it's what she likes. She doesn't want an iPhone. She got the Huawei for twenty euro on a special offer. She likes the screen. All she uses it for is making phone calls and texting. Or so I believe. My dad hates it. He is embarrassed if she uses it in company. See-saw, Margery Daw. He goes up, she comes down. My fucking life I swear.

I went up to my brother's room and knocked on the door. There was no answer so I went in. Like our family is obsessed about privacy except for my mam walking into the bathroom when I'm peeing which is meant to be a girl thing. Not. It's like everything is private except the most embarrassing thing. Once she even saw me changing my pad ffs. But we never go into each other's rooms.

He was still asleep. Some time during the night he kicked the duvet off. He was lying on the bed in his underpants and I could see that there were scars on his legs but they were old scars, very old, and not very many.

I had more already. So that was why he gave me the razors. The bastard. But there were bruises on his ribs, dark blue-black circles with wine-coloured spots in the centre. And there were bruises on his arms. And his nose looked all right this morning even though it was a bit swollen and there was blood around the rim. But what really shocked me was how fit he looked. Like he must have been working out. I never knew he went to the gym. He had abs and biceps and all the rest of it. He was like a wounded god. For the first time ever I saw that my brother was beautiful. I guess my mam always knew. She has always been in love with him. I blushed. I don't know why. I backed out of the room and closed the door.

It was Serena who found out where my dad was living. Clarinda Park, where we had an empty house. He wasn't living with Miss Morocco idk maybe she wouldn't have him. By then my mam had her mobile switched off. She wasn't texting him and she wasn't speed-dialling him any more. Her heart had hardened. When a heart gets too hard it just breaks. Mine was breaking too. I could feel it. I spent four days shaking and thinking where is my dad? What if he dies and I'm not there? Like that's the other side of, What if he dies when I'm there? Idk. I'm confused. Then I was just sad. Holly and Serena told me stories. Like your dad is hiding out from the Revenue. Your dad is gone somewhere to get money to pay them off. Fairytales. It wasn't the money. So after school one day me and Serena and Holly went to Clarinda Park. Holly does German and French. She hates Miss Philpott. Like one time Holly made a mistake in grammar and Miss Philpott said there was no place in the German language for stupidity. Like what the actual fuck? Does that even mean anything? Holly says having a teacher who is a Nazi is normal. *C'est la vie*, she says. She says, At least I'm not Greek. I don't get that and neither does

Serena. But as we were walking Holly did the names of the roads in a German accent. Like, Emperley, Eshley, Villowmere, Eshley Mound, Kinksvay, Ze Pattocks, Vyndham Cloze, Eshley Cloze. And then she makes a sort of orgasmic sound. And then, Oh Kenzinkton Downz, Brrrrierly Downz, Entzleigh, Clarinda Park. Her and Serena thought it was hilarious and I laughed too, but inside I was just sad. Then she was taking off Angela Merkel. She can do Angela Merkel like she was real. Leary hates Merkel. Holly can do languages, it's her thing. She says she is going to learn a new language every five years. Next up is Italian. Emperley is Amberley. Only knobs live there. Like every second house is Inhabited By An Executive Of A Fortune 500 Company with Electric Gates and Cameras. I imagine him sitting in his office watching us going by on his mobile phone. We try to see if the cameras track us but they are maybe fixed cameras. That's the bargain-basement option. The real deal is cameras you can control yourself. Like imagine you're on holidays in Bermuda or wherever Fortune 500 guys go to chill, and you're sitting by the pool with some totally hot blonde and you're on your gold-plated iPhone watching some skanky langer in a tracksuit and a ski mask breaking in your back window and nicking your kit. A camera would ruin a trip to Bermuda.

After Amberley comes Ashley. Business people and comfortable professionals. Electric gates, no cameras. Then it's downhill all the way, geographically and economically. At the very bottom, where my dad puts his money, Clarinda Park is for students and people with JobBridge internships and immigrants. My dad specialises in skangers. His business model is heavily dependent on Rent Supplement and the Household Benefits Package and the Student Assistance Fund. It was a new trend he spotted right at the beginning of The Crash. He was an early adopter.

Clarinda Park was two lines of twenty houses, four of them empty and boarded up. The road was bad, like so many potholes, mostly stones as white as bone. There was only one functioning streetlight and a few places where they planned to put more before The Crash. Like poles with no lights, or holes with no poles. There were also eight houses that were not boarded up that had no furniture in them. I said to Holly, This is what they call a ghost estate. Like we did that 'Ghost Estate' poem in Fifth. If you lived here you'd be home by now idk I'm not sure I got it. She said this place was too young to have ghosts. And I said, You can have ghosts at any age. My dad's car wasn't there but he would finish at the office in an hour, except I was in the office twice looking for him and they said he wasn't in. So he wasn't going to the office. Which is like The Nuclear Option. It was a warm day with a blue sky. We went round the back. There were patio chairs and a table. The garden was all ratty grass. No plants. There was a timber fence about a metre high. His washing was on the clothes line, three underpants, two vests, four shirts and a pair of pants. No socks. Idk it was sad. At home my dad was always complaining that my brother stole his socks, but it was usually just one of a pair that was missing so idk. I wondered if they went missing in Clarinda Park too.

A neighbour came out to her garden and asked us if we were OK. Like if we were burglars or winos we would just sit around on the patio for a couple of hours. I said I was waiting for my dad to get home. She gave me a sad look. Did we want a cup of tea? We said no thanks. Serena asked her to take a pic of the three of us on her phone. She gave her the phone. It was a top of the range iPhone. Serena is the kind of person who has her phone insured. The woman took a pic and gave it back. She went back inside. She was watching telly, we could see her sitting on a couch with her back to the window. The couch was huge. There was some kind of food programme on. All that was in the room was a forty-eight inch flat screen and a couch. It was like no humans need apply.

My dad houses were always Fully Furnished To A High Standard, one-hundred-per-cent IKEA, with All Appliances Including Microwave because my dad said unfurnished houses gave tenants more rights. My dad is Against Tenant Rights. In History he would have been a landlord and he would have been against the Land League which everyone is agreed was a good thing. Michael Davitt is a hero in Irish history because he won tenant rights, Fair Rent, Fixity Of Tenure, Free Sale. I think that's partly because he had one arm. Wounded people are often heroes. Our History teacher told us that he was a friend of Karl Marx's sister or daughter. Like that's not much. It's like saying, A friend of a friend knows Somebody Important. Like the seven degrees of separation. But seven degrees is too much and there is no way the guy in the seventh degree is going to help you out of trouble. Like I might be seven degrees from Barack Obama but if I write to him with a bullet point list of how we're only seven degrees apart, is he going to come over here and tell my parents to get together again and stop fighting before they kill us all?

Maybe Michael Davitt was a friend of Karl Marx too, the way Tosser is a friend of mine because he's a friend of my brother, but history does not record.

My dad's car drove up at twenty minutes past five. We waited until he got inside and saw us through the patio door. Holly started to blush but Serena just looked from him to me. She was curious about how people who shouted would act together. He opened the sliding door and said, Hi, girls. Serena said, Hi. Holly said, Hi, Mr Regan. I said, Hi, Dad.

We stood there looking at each other for a bit. Then I went in and closed the patio door. My dad didn't say anything because he knew why I was there. I knew what his first thought was so I told him. Mam didn't send me, Dad, and she doesn't know I'm here.

He gave me a look like a hurt dog. Like The Dog gives me when I shout at him, or there's shouting in the house. He hates arguments. So that started me crying. I couldn't stop and I put my hands over my face. And after a bit I felt his arms around me. Idk when he last put his arms around me, maybe I was a baby. We stood there like that, not saying anything, and all the while I knew Serena was watching me to see how it's done. After a while my dad said, If I come home what will your mam say?

I don't know.

I don't either.

She was ringing you like crazy the first two days but you never answered.

I needed to work things out.

So what did you work out, Dad?

He stepped away from me. I wasn't crying now. He was staring at the window. I saw Holly sitting with her back turned and Serena staring straight in. Jason Clancy was texting Holly for a date. She got eleven texts in four days. I just knew she was replying to another one. She had that pissed-off texting look to her shoulders. Jason is a one hundred per cent langer. Even Holly sees that.

That Serena has no manners, he said.

What did you work out, Dad?

Nothing.

I said, Can we have a cup of tea? We came straight from school.

How did you know I was here?

Is this the only house we own here?

He waved to Holly and Serena. He opened the patio door for them. Want a cup of tea, girls? I have biscuits.

Yes please, Mr Regan, Serena said, smiling like fucking the devil Annabelle the doll in *The Conjuring*. They came in.

My friend Serena, all sweetness and light. Miss Sweetie herself. FFS.

Tea and biscuits, my dad said, and then I'll drive you home.

Serena brushed against him as she came in and then looked up at him and smiled and said, Sorry, Mr Regan.

My dad looked at me. He knew I saw. She makes me sick.

My mam had her phone in her hand like she was going to ring someone, the guards or the ambulance or even my dad. She was leaning against the kitchen sink. She was looking at my dad. My dad was looking at her. Then she started to slap her phone against the palm of her other hand. There was a flock of birds on the purple tree in our garden. It was directly behind my mam and I could see them tearing something off. Maybe buds or flowers. Do birds eat buds? They were just ripping things and throwing them away. She said, There's letters for you, I would have forwarded them but I didn't have an address, they're from the Revenue, I got them too.

Dad: What do they say?

Mam: They want us to come in again. My solicitor says they're going to declare us bankrupt.

Dad: Your solicitor?

Mam: That's what she said.

Dad: When did she make this pronouncement? How long have you been talking to her about me?

My mam sighed. Then she turned around and ran the cold tap. Then she took a glass out of the cupboard and filled it with cold water. Then she drank it. All of it, all the way down, a whole glass of water in one go. It's a family tradition in my house, drinking water when you're stressed. Other people go for the drinks cabinet, but with us it's the cold tap. Except my dad who needs alcohol in everything. This may be because all our best fights happen in the kitchen and there is no drinks cabinet to hand. They seemed to have forgotten about me. Then she turned around again.

I asked you months ago, she said, and you said everything was fine, we were back on our feet again, the houses were paying. You said we'd turned the corner.

What fucking corner? There's no corners. It's just one long road.

Downhill.

My dad shrugged. You were happy enough in the good times.

Matt, she said, I was never happy. You are a complete shit, you are now and you always were. I was sorry I married you on the day I married you and nothing has changed. There were never good times.

That's what you say now, but you usen't to say it. You're only saying it because of the Revenue.

I asked my solicitor if I divorced you now would I still be liable and she said I would.

You asked her about if you divorced me?

She said I would carry the debt with me the same as I would carry the property. Half and half.

Your fucking solicitor? She couldn't write a postcard nevermind a fucking divorce letter. I warned you she was a bimbo, a complete airhead. She's a blonde for fuck's sake.

You'll find out soon enough if she's an airhead. She'll be writing to you. She'll be looking for discovery of documents. I have a right to them as a director. Get on to Molloy and remind him you donated at the last election.

I already did. He told me it was the Revenue and he had his own share of worries. You know that old-folks home that was on the telly? He's a director there. Non-Exec.

He's a useless fucker anyway, my mam said. He'd only screw everything up.

My father sat down at the kitchen table. In the window behind his head I saw two blue-tits making out, or at least thinking about making out. They were flying around each other the way you can make two hands turn around each other. Like if you were cold. But they were excited. Spring was beginning. It was all happening for them.

You want me to go again? he said.

She looked at him and then she seemed to notice me. She looked at me for an awful long time. I held my breath until I had to let it go. Then she said, No. Stay if you like.

I heard him breathing again too. He said, We'll work something out.

I'm going to the Revenue separately. I'm going to make my own case. You can do your silence routine for yourself, but I'm going to hang you. You're the one who didn't pay your tax, not me.

Then everything seemed to be good again idk they didn't fight. It was like restructuring was in progress. A new and better kind of Mam and Dad. But after a few days I started to worry that there was no fighting. It was unnatural. And my dad was like a zombie. Not like a zombie because of drugs. It was just he didn't seem to react to anything. Like he was cold idk or somewhere else. Once I swear I saw him park the car in the drive outside and bounce his head off the steering wheel twice. It's a leather-coated wheel though, so I don't think he did much damage. There is something wrong I know.

Is there like a time when you're grown up when you know what's going on? When it's not so scary?

Another time I saw him in the bathroom. He was standing at the sink just looking at himself in the mirror. The door was open. He didn't see me. I don't know how long he was standing there.

In bed I'd listen all the time they were downstairs and when they went up I listened for as long as I could stay awake. I knew I shouldn't listen.

Sometimes I would hear low talking. Like people making clandestine plans. Or people with something terrible to say.

How was I supposed to know? Like I'm seventeen years-of-age. How Am I Supposed To Know Anything?

I think they were both taking my dad's sleeping pills. Or else my mam got her own supply. Our doctor would prescribe cocaine if you asked him. If the pharmacy stocked it. By the end of the week I couldn't sleep. I was lying awake listening to the silence. I'd hear my brother come in. Sometimes The Dog barked at him. I would say, As soon as Tony is asleep I'll fall asleep too. But it's one thing you can't wait for or expect. Eventually I slogged one of dad's pills and that night was a Saturday night and I slept until after twelve on Sunday.

And the next morning was the Monday that my dad told me their secret plan. The Revenue were going to serve some notice on him and he needed to be out of sight. We were all going to go to this house that was owned by a friend of his way Out In The Wilderness idk Kerry or somewhere. A holiday cottage. We stayed in holiday cottages before. They're OK. Him and me would go first and get the place warmed up. We would be joined by Mam and Tony as soon as she got out of work. We were going to lie low there because the Revenue would not be able to serve a summons which has to be done in person. The way Dad talked we were the French Resistance. We were headed for the hills and the Gestapo would never find us. I was to pack my bag that night and leave it under my bed and he would pick me up from school during the day on Tuesday. He would say I had a doctor's appointment. Then we would disappear into the hills and forests until the war was over. I said, Dad this is like absconding. It seemed to me that my dad's answer to everything was to hide out somewhere for a while. I had a bad feeling we were all moving into Clarinda Park and that was his real secret plan. Jesus wept for the third time. It was complete crap.

Me: Dad, are you OK? Like I'm worried about you. Are you depressed?

Dad: Oh for God's sake, Suzy, stop googling everything.

Me: I didn't google it, Dad. I'm just worried.

But actually I did google it. My dad is acting weird, hitting his head, walking around like a zombie, not talking, taking sleeping pills. I got: Learn First Aid for psychosis; Symptoms of substance-induced psychotic disorder; I feel like I'm losing my mind, I beg of you to reply; My life as an Ambien Zombie. It turns out that Ambien is a sedative used in the short-term treatment of insomnia. I got one point one million hits. That's Google.

Me: Are you and Mam going to break up?

Dad: Don't be ridiculous.

Me: What's going on?

Dad: I told you what's going on. We're going to lie low for a while.

Me: We're absconding. I know it. You should talk to someone, Dad.

Dad: No, it's only absconding if the summons has been served.

Me: Did you ask your solicitor about this?

Dad: You can't ask a solicitor about something like that. I googled it.

I could see my dad sitting in his car googling summonses and absconding on his mobile. Five billion hits. All from people who successfully absconded up to that point. No updates because the whole bunch are in a prison where they don't get WiFi. Like, maybe just one of them might have said, Guys, be cool, this is not a good idea, it's illegal, you could end up in gaol. But it would be hit number five billion and one. My dad is not the brightest idk it's like he has a money brain but no real brain. They say entrepreneurs are geniuses, you hear it on the radio, like do you want to affirm and reward these unique individuals, Ernst & Young Entrepreneur Of The Year and all that shite, but you don't have be a genius to make money out of money, you just need a brass neck. And once you have money the dodgy chancers come round like bees to honey. I think he loved my mam, but did she love him, idk, maybe? You can't believe everything she says.

I decided I had to go with him because otherwise he'd lose it completely. He needed someone to take care of him and it looked like that someone was me.

The most scariest thing my dad said to me that Sunday? I have everything under control, Suzy, just relax.

The only person I told was Holly because you couldn't tell Serena. And anyway Serena was obsessed by Graham Dwyer and why he had handcuffs and stuff.

Holly thought it was a great idea. Screw the law, she said, you'd be like outlaws, guerrillas, Robin Hood and his Merry Men. I want to come too. My daddy and mammy would love it.

Holly's dad is a bit involved with the protests about the evictions. Holly and me agreed that no matter what our dads did we would stay friends forever. It turns out her dad is in a political party that's not up for evicting people for non-payment. They're not Blue, Green or Pink. Maybe they're Red or Black, Holly doesn't know about the colours. My mam thinks he's the Antichrist. Like the Antichrist must be a commie or an anarchist, it just makes complete sense. If my mam was around in Christ's time she would have said he was the Antichrist. And they stopped my dad doing an eviction one day. They all stood around outside and the sheriff didn't want to risk it. My dad wants them all in jail.

Dad says I'm not even supposed to mention absconding to my mam because seemingly my mam is too scared of the idea. But she's going to do it. She Will Join Us Later.

That doesn't sound like your mam, Holly said.

That's what my dad said. She was so nervous she didn't want to talk about it.

Sounds to me like your dad is fucking kidnapping you. Like that's what paedophiles say. It's just our secret. You should have told your mam.

My dad is not a paedophile for fuck's sake.

I'm not saying he is.

And anyway Mam is gone to work.

Phone her. Tell her.

My dad would kill me.

Well, don't say I didn't warn you if he cuts you up and stores your bits in the deep freeze.

We were waiting at our bus stop. There was that dribbly rain that's a bit heavier than mist but not fully grown rain. It was pissy. And it was cold too. The weather forecast said the air mass was coming from the continent where they were getting a nasty patch, people dying in their cars in snowdrifts. There was a weather warning yellow, wintry showers turning to snow over high ground. A danger of heavier falls in mountainous areas of the West. It never snowed enough. Ireland is a crap country for weather. Everything we get is wet.

Don't tell them in school. You'll get into trouble.

You know me. I won't tell.

I knew she wouldn't. They could waterboard Holly and she would never talk. I had the feeling she was right but I thought I owed my dad. I had to give him a chance. Like, I was the only one on his side.

I don't know how long I'll be gone, I said.

Holly gulped suddenly, like a huge gulp. And then she threw her arms around me and kissed me. She kissed me right on the lips and I kissed her back. I think she was a bit surprised about that. But she stuck it out. Two resistors connected in parallel. Name an instrument for measuring resistance. Calculate the current flowing in the circuit. Potential difference. I could have stayed connected forever. We were a long time doing it. The two of us were crying and hugging each other. It was the best feeling. I love Holly. When she stopped kissing me she said, Stay safe.

You too.

Then our bus came.

Naturally it wasn't a holiday cottage. It was a shitty cottage. Jesus wept twice. A wannabe holiday home by the sea. But it was halfway to ruin and the sea was a long way down. What kind of a friend of my dad's thought this shack was a holiday cottage? I didn't know he had such dodgy friends. Well, I knew he had dodgy friends but they were all builders and auctioneers. The walls were made of stone and they were a metre thick. The floor was concrete. The facilities comprised of: lounge (concrete floor), kitchen (pine, ancient manky cooker with like iron rings, decorative sprinkling of mouse shit), bathroom with shower (no heating, tiled floor), master bedroom on the ground floor at the back, mezzanine bedroom. A mezzanine bedroom where I was supposed to sleep. I hate sleeping if people can see me. Like even on school tours I never wanted to sleep with someone else. The walls were bare stone hundreds of years old. I don't know what lived in the cracks. There was a big iron stove in the lounge, two ratty couches and a woodwormed table with four woodwormed chairs. The wormholes could have been fakes, I saw a documentary about that once. There was one window in every room but they were all small. The floor of my room was pine boards and my bed was pine and there was an old pine trunk as a bedside table. And all the pine was mainly woodworm, more holes than wood, mostly air and dust and whatever woodworms look like, maybe not worms at all. The trunk was empty except for woodworm. I put my clothes in it. My fucking life.

But on the very first evening a man knocked at our door to sell us turf. He saw the light, he said, though he didn't mention where he saw it from. He must have been hanging around on the edge of some cliff or up the mountain. His name was Peter. I suspect he saw a car passing and when it didn't come back he loaded up the van and drove out just in case. We bought two bags at six euro a bag. Peter wanted to talk. He stood half-in, half-out, not looking at us except every now and then when he wanted to check how we were reacting. The wind howled past him. The inside started to feel like the outside. And the outside was the North Pole. He told us the house was built before the famine, that once upon a time a hundred people lived up here on this side of the cliff, and further out there was another empty village and a hundred and twenty-two people lived out there and now there was one and he was an old man and a cranky man at that, and sure all the young people were gone from this place, America, Australia, England, it was only all old people were left, dying away one by one, since The Crash nearly everyone left, no work, no money in the fishing or the farming, no one wants to be

171

on the dole all their life, you couldn't make the land pay around here, it was mostly bog, even the sheep got foot-rot and maggots were as common as flies, you couldn't even cut turf without a licence, it was like the famine all over again only they weren't hungry or they weren't too hungry anyway and nobody was paying their fare to America, but every second house was empty, and those that had inhabitants lost someone every winter, for it is winter that kills the old people, only for that they would live forever around here, his own neighbour, a young man who had a bit of a farm and who was only two fields away, came in one morning and handed him the key of the house, Look after that for me, Peter, he says, I'm off to Australia, I'll be back in a year, didn't he have a job in the mining in Adelaide or wherever they had the mining, his cousin set him up with it.

My dad wanted to get rid of him. I could see it. He has no patience for talk. But he couldn't find a place to say something. Peter just kept talking without looking. Every now and again he would take a step closer to the door and then he would take the same step back again. It was like a dance. Sometimes it was two steps. I wanted him to stay because I was scared of what would happen when the door would close and it would just be us.

He gave us his mobile number in case we burned through the turf before our holiday was up. It was good dry stuff, he said, maybe too dry some of them were saying. It was all machine cutting now, the machine did no damage at all, and it had a sort of hose out the side to spit out the turf. I had no idea what he was talking about. He had a Ford van. He got back into it eventually and waved and drove away.

What an asshole, my dad said.

And after that it was just me and him. We lit the stove. I don't know why, but that first evening we were happy. There was no television or radio but my dad found a pack of cards in a drawer and we played poker and snap and beggar-my-neighbour until bed time. It is hard for two people to play cards. My mam did not come that night. And neither did Tony.

The next morning my dad didn't wake. I knew he had his sleeping pills so I let him sleep. I could hear him snoring. I made a slice of toast. And then I went out. It was a fine morning, sunny and warm. Or at least it was not cold. I climbed up behind the house and had a look around. About four kilometres away to the north I saw the first house, down below in the valley and close to the shore. There was smoke coming out of the chimney and Peter's van was parked outside. The sea was empty. There were no fishing boats. I saw sheep and one or two cattle. I thought, ffs we're off the edge of the map. This was the middle of nowhere, in fact it was the outside edge of nowhere. We were inhabiting an uninhabited peninsula on a temporary basis and America was our next-door neighbour. There was just my dad and me. By then I didn't think my mam was coming, and I knew Tony wasn't. Tony liked his comfort. One of the ratty couches was convertible.

I couldn't see Tony sleeping on it. And my mam would miss the gym and the aircon.

My mam would be talking to her solicitor already. She would have a good story for the Revenue: Her husband ran away to a place or places unknown, she didn't. Evading his responsibilities. How long would it take them to find him?

That time I decided that my dad was a stupid bastard, a selfish bastard. I thought about walking down to Peter's house and getting him to drive me to the nearest bus stop. If they had bus stops in this shithole of a place.

So my dad crashed idk he stayed in bed all next morning and he wouldn't eat unless I cooked. I'm a crap cook as my mam Never Tires Of Telling Me and my dad can't boil an egg. And I was paranoid about the mice even though I never saw one personally. I put everything in the fridge, even the tea. And at night sometimes I would hear them running. Or I would think I could hear a sound like a million needles clittering somewhere between my floor and the ceiling below. Maybe they were ghost mice, ex-mice that died in the famine. Or did the mice have plenty to eat, maybe it was only a human disaster and the mice and rats had a fun few years. Then again maybe they were bionic woodlice. The first night I fried a steak. I didn't fry it enough and when we cut it the blood leaked. I freaked. I put mine back on the pan and left it there until it was black on the outside, but still when I cut there was that dribble of blood. I wanted to put an Elastoplast on it before I put it in the bin. So I just ate toast and oven chips. On the second day I made an omelette and it was OK. There is no blood in an omelette.

I said, Dad we have no food for tomorrow, just the stale bread.

He gave me fifty euro.

I'm like: Where am I supposed to find something?

But he didn't answer. By then he wasn't talking much. He stayed in bed until his tea was ready and then he got up and ate it and went back to bed again. He was taking a pill in the morning now too. I thought maybe it would be good for his heart. They say rest is good. In the Shakespeare we were doing in school someone says, Sleep that knits up the ravel'd sleeve of care, balm of hurt minds idk that's what I thought at the time and if I changed my mind it was afterwards. Otherwise I would have got him out of the bed every morning.

So I walked down to Peter's house with my fifty euro. I knocked on his door and he let me in. He made me tea. His house was nice idk it was warm and there were two comfortable chairs and an open fire. He was burning his own turf, I saw. I asked him about a shop and he said the nearest shop was eleven miles away, my dad would have to drive me. I said my dad wasn't well and he was sleeping a lot, he had a stent put in. Peter said the stent was mighty, his own brother had one, before he was hardly able to stand up out of a chair and afterwards he was taking long walks on the beach every day. I said my dad was mostly asleep all day. He had sleeping pills they gave him. Peter said nothing. We drank our tea.

I'll drive you out to the town, he said.

I said I didn't want to put him to any trouble.

Sure I have to go out anyway, I have to go to the Post Office.

His favourite TV programmes were *Masterchef* and *Strictly Come Dancing*. *Strictly* was brilliant the way you had these leggers who couldn't put one foot in front of the other and at the end of the series they could dance on an egg-box. That was the whole thing about it, the sense of achievement. Ballroom dancing was all the rage when he was a youngster. The priests didn't like it of course, but them boys were against anything. If the clergy had their way there wouldn't be a child born in Ireland from the coming of St Patrick to the present time. Supposedly they were against it because it was foreign. Great saviours of the Gaelic way of life were the clergy. But sure wasn't the Latin foreign too? And Christianity itself? It's not like Jesus started his ministry in a bog in the West of Ireland. And if he did, things would have taken a different turn and there might have been less burning at the stake. It's very hard to set fire to a person with turf.

I liked to hear Peter laughing.

It's lonely enough at times, he said, as we turned into the village. And sure if you ever think of marrying a bachelor farmer with a pension when you grow up, you have my mobile.

And the two of us laughed over that again. But he might have been serious idk. And if he was, I wasn't against it either. I could think of a lot worse. Like once I saw Leary our history teacher on a date. He was with a woman. He had on a tweed jacket exactly the same as the one he wears in class but cleaner. He had the same pair of pants he wears in class. We don't think he changes it, but maybe he bought five pairs at the start. His shoes had a shine on them. He opened his car door for the woman. Like his car is this half-Renault half-Datsun, I don't even know if it has a name, maybe just a number like fourteen. Datsuns are hip now if you can get one, they all rotted. But I was also bizarrely like so jealous, a little bit idk not much but it was there. Leary must be over forty. Maybe it's because he's History. The woman looked like a teacher too, kinda smart idk Primary maybe, with glasses. I was hoping they'd make it together. Leary is lonely and I am attracted to lonely old guys.

I would not invite Serena to the wedding, I could imagine what she'd say.

I went to the SuperValu and I bought a super-giant bag of frozen peas, three packets of lamb chops totalling twelve chops in all, a giant bag of oven chips and a few sliced pans. Peter told me the trick of the sliced pan was to freeze it and soften it in the toaster as you wanted it. That way you could have fresh bread for a long time. He drove me back up to my house. We didn't have a toaster but I froze the bread anyway.

Listen, girl, he said, call me any time, or come down for a cup of tea. Don't be a stranger now.

I nearly cried. But I didn't.

I missed Holly and Serena. I missed kissing Holly. That was the best. I missed my bedroom. I was scared all night here, like the place had to be haunted. Even if no ghost turned up just yet, there would be one sooner or later. Probably some long-dead bogman trying to sell me a load of ghost turf. Like people must have died here during the famine. I could see these hungry bastards tapping at my window and demanding to be fed, like it was hard enough cooking for my dad. And as far as I knew, they only ate potatoes and I was shit at boiling potatoes, I always boiled them to mush or else they were hard. The bathroom was freezing and you couldn't lock the door and I was scared my dad was going to wake up and walk in on me. He wouldn't even know where he was. And I was expecting my period and I forgot to bring pads and I couldn't ask Peter to drive me into town for them. And I was scared my dad was going to die in his sleep like you do. And other times I felt like going down and putting a pillow over his face and sitting on it until he stopped kicking. The bastard.

He kidnapped me. The bastard. I hate my father. I swear.

Dad, I said one breakfast time, maybe the third morning, I lost track of time, What's Mam saying? Is she coming down?

He didn't look at me. That was a bad sign. I said, Did you talk to her? Or is it just texts?

Nothing, he said.

What, she like just didn't reply?

He looked at the stove. The turf was burning bright. It was like he saw it for the first time. He put his head on one side and then the other. It was comical idk maybe.

Dad?

I threw the phone in a bin before I left the office.

What? Why?

They can trace you. I saw it in a court case in the papers. Triangulation.

So Mam doesn't know where we are? Right, Dad? She doesn't know and she thinks we just disappeared. Maybe she thinks we went to England? Maybe she thinks we're dead? Like that suicide a year ago, the guy that drove into the sea with his two children.

He shrugged. Those kids were only toddlers.

Like is that better? It's OK to drive into the sea with a pair of toddlers?

He looked blank. I could see he wasn't exactly following my argument. And then I realised that I wasn't following it either.

I said, Are you thinking of driving into the sea? Because if you are you can forget about me coming along. Like I just won't be there. That sea is cold. Take a look at it some time.

She's going to hang me out to dry.

Dad what's happening? I don't know what's happening.

He shrugged again. Nothing.

He got up and went into his bedroom. After maybe twenty seconds in there he closed the door. Then I heard his bed creaking. I knocked on the door. There was no answer so I went in. He was lying on the flat of his back with the duvet pulled up to his chin. Like it wasn't even a cold day. There was a fresh blister-pack on the bedside table with one blister punched out. There was a sour smell, like bad breath. He didn't look at me.

So this is not about the Revenue? This is about Mam, right, Dad? This is about making her pay?

He closed his eyes.

For fuck's sake, I said, I legit hate this place. What are we doing here?

He never even told me legit was not a word. He had his eyes closed and he never opened them once. For the first time ever I noticed that he had really long lashes, like a girl's.

I hate you, I said.

181

I went out of the room again. I slammed the door behind me but it didn't slam because it doesn't fit the frame properly. It just sort whooshed and closed and then drifted open a bit. I sat down at the kitchen table and tried to think. He obviously never thought about my phone. I could just call my mam and tell her where we were and what was going on. Except there's no signal. My phone is showing No Service, the understatement of the century so far.

And then I thought he's not that stupid, he knows I have a phone. I'm meant to call Mam and tell her. He wants me to tell her.

I texted Holly, My dad is gone into hibernation.

Holly: Like seriously does he have enough nuts?

Me: He's not a squirrel.

Holly: I no.

And then I thought, He's depressed, classic symptoms, won't talk, won't get out of bed, abusing pills. It's A CRY FOR HELP. We got all that in Health Ed. We saw a video. It was about a guy drawing on a big sheet of wood. It was crap. Signs To Look Out For. Is Your Friend Depressed Or Suicidal? How To Help. The advice was always Contact Somebody. There was a list of people you could contact: a priest, a doctor, a teacher, a guidance counsellor. We had no guidance counsellors any more, they were abolished after The Crash. You were supposed to get your advice from the telly or Google. The only person I could think of was Peter. And he wasn't on the list.

So Peter made me tea again. He had some nice chocolate biscuits. He had a sweet tooth for the bikkies, he said, sure it could be worse. I asked him about his books. They were two kinds, he said: books in Irish and westerns. I could see he was reading one called *Kill Dusty Fog*. He said the western was dead as a doornail, you could not buy one now, the last one he bought was one called *Brokeback Mountain*, somebody told him it was about cowboys, but it was useless, it was written by a woman of course, and women could not do westerns whatever else they could do, so he just read the old ones over and over again, the funny thing was he could never recall the endings until he got to the end, but he had a good idea who would live and who would die, that's the important thing, there's nothing worse than the hero dying, it's very hard altogether, but if you knew it was going to happen you could be prepared for it, then it wasn't so bad. And what about the Irish books? They were his mother's, she was a school teacher back in Bolus, it was the old National School, she was a native Irish speaker and he grew up with it himself, his favourite book of all was *Dánta Ghrádha* collected by Thomas F. O'Rahilly with a foreword by Robin Flower, they were all in the old Irish of course, you'd have to work hard to understand that kind of thing, but what else would he be doing? and it was interesting to see how those old people managed the courting business, it was very intricate altogether and they had beautiful words like *rún* and *searc*, we don't have at all in the English the like of it, it was not like nowadays when you could go on the internet and buy a wife from Latvia, he knew a man who bought his from there, if you could believe it, and it worked out well enough too, although she was thirty years his junior, he left her a fine house and a Ford Focus, it was a B&B now, the Latvians are hard workers, in his father's time there was matchmaking of course, and in a way that was the internet for them, you would put out word that you were wanting a wife and a wife would be found and if the two of you agreed well enough that was the match made, it was better than the lonesomeness anyway, and his own mother used to say even if you had an old dog around the house you'd get fond of him after a while, which was not a bad saying for it worked both ways, the man for the woman and the woman for the man, the women were masters of the house anyway, so it was more important for the man to get on with the woman or he would get thin gruel morning, noon and night, a bitter woman in the house was the worst thing of all, even a bitter man wasn't as bad for he was out of the house from the dawn with work to do, but a bitter woman soured everything, they had their ways, of course, and the man could go rambling at night-time, he would go card-playing or dancing from house to house, a man with a good voice was always welcome for they were mighty people for songs, if you could sing and you knew a share of songs there would always be a welcome, and if there was a welcome there would be drink, many a man was turned into a raving alcoholic by night-rambling, even men that started out sober young fellows, by the end of it they would be a pity.

Are you married, Peter?

Never married, he said, never worried, never wed, never fed.

I'd say Peter could talk for Ireland. All I had to do was drink my tea and eat my biscuits. But it was idk OK. He was OK. While he talked I looked at things. He had a picture over the fireplace that must have been his mother. She looked like a nice woman. She was standing beside a door that was like the door of a school. She was smiling. He had a painting on another wall of birds flying over mud. He had a bookshelf. There was an antique kind of sideboard thing with willow-pattern plates. There was a big round basket full of turf.

When the tea was finished he made another pot and more biscuits came out, different ones but still chocolate. It was maybe after an hour that he said to me, What ails you, child? What has you down today?

And then I didn't know what to say. I was trying to think where to start. I looked in on my dad before I left and he was thrown on the bed snoring. Thunder and lightning wouldn't wake him.

I don't know, I said. Like if my dad is not well?

Why didn't you say so from the get go? Does he need a doctor?

I don't know, I said, I think maybe it's like depression. I don't know. Maybe.

He was just going to drink his tea. He had the cup to his lips. He stopped doing it. Very slowly he put the cup back on the saucer. He said something in Irish. My Irish is crap really. It's not bad for reading but I'm crap at listening tests.

Then he goes: Has he the darkness on him?

That took me by surprise. It was so beautiful. I didn't know there was a beautiful way of saying it like everybody just says depression or mood.

I said I didn't know, that he was just sleeping all the time, that he took sleeping pills.

The poor man. Did he only take the prescribed dosage though?

I said I didn't know what my dad was doing. I didn't know what was going on. I thought he was running away from my mother because they were going to split up, that he tricked me into coming too, also that he was maybe running away from debts, that I was worried about him, and I was worried about my family, and my brother was in trouble too. I was worried that maybe he wanted to kill himself too or something idk. Maybe. I don't know what's going on. I don't know what else I said. He listened to me.

Then he said, My daddy was locked up, in the asylum beyond. He was cracked from whiskey.

I didn't know what to say. I was looking at the cover of *Kill Dusty Fog*. I was wondering if cowboys ever got depressed. You never heard about it. Maybe they hadn't the time.

Peter said, He would be gone for a week or more, drinking wherever he could get drink. He would take cattle to the fair of Kenmare and not come back until he drank the money. He was a terror for it. Then he'd be recovering for a few weeks and then he'd start again. What he died of was cirrhosis of the liver and he died in the asylum. Only for my mother's wages we would be destitute altogether. He died roaring. If anyone had it coming he had.

Don't say that, I said. It's too sad. He was your daddy.

I was thinking that if my dad went bankrupt there would only be my mother's salary. That my dad would die if he couldn't make money because money was all he ever thought about. It was his one and only skill. It was his secret baby.

I'm not saying that your father is going the same way.

He's not. He hardly drinks at all.

He nodded. He was watching me. He had small quick eyes but they were bright enough. He was a very tall man but he was shy. Now when he was watching me he was doing it sideways, out of the corners of his eyes.

We had a bit of a farm back in the valley there, he said, and my daddy drank it. He drank the farm and he drank the house and when he was locked up roaring and shouting for seeing things my mother packed up and moved down here to the seaside. She got a job teaching because her husband was in the asylum and the priest

189

took pity on her. It was a shame in those days to have someone in the madhouse. People said she drove him mad, would you believe that? They always say that sort of thing. They have to blame someone. But he did it himself. When he was sober he was a nice man. He used to play pitch and toss with me.

I said that my friend's daddy made a splint out of matchsticks for a robin with a broken leg and afterwards the robin used to come inside their house during cold weather. Peter said the leg probably troubled the robin and the cold made it worse. His own knee troubled him when it was wet.

Would you come up and look at my dad? Like I don't know if he's safe to leave alone.

I will. I'll drive you back up. Finish your tea and we'll go.

I said I couldn't drink any more.

So he drove me up and we went into the bedroom and looked at him. And he never woke up even though there was a strange man standing at the foot of his bed. Peter brought a smell of turf smoke with him. And he said my dad was bad all right, that kind of sleep was unnatural, and I should get a doctor in the morning if he's not better. But I knew I couldn't do that. If I called a doctor he might be reported. Or they might send him into the asylum if they still had asylums idk. I promised Peter I would call a doctor first thing and he went home. And by then it was dark. It gets dark early in February even though we were as far west as you could go without falling into the sea. The sun sets behind the mountain so there's a shadow over us from early. My book was finished and I had nothing to read. I should have borrowed something from Peter. I started googling stuff and I got sad because googling depression is bad. So I watched YouTube videos instead even though it would eat up my credit. I saw Zombie Make Up Tips. It was brilliant. How to do your face like a zombie with basically household ingredients every kitchen should have. Like I'm talking about gelatine and porridge and jam. I cooked some lamb chops and peas and I boiled potatoes, but I had to eat it all myself because my dad said he didn't want anything. He was getting thin and I was getting fat.

And that was the hardest night ever. There was a wet gale blowing with hailstones. It was like someone slinging gravel at the windows. And the doors rattled and the wind got in everywhere and it was seriously cold. You could hear the gale grumbling and growling in the stove. Every time there was a gust something else caught fire in there.

I was so lonely. I missed Holly and Serena and I missed my brother. I kept going over and over everything. What I wanted most of all was to cut but I didn't bring my razors. I forgot them leaving the house. I thought about the carving knife but it was too blunt. There was a bread knife with a serrated edge but I thought that would make shit of my leg. I didn't want to bleed to death while my dad was asleep. Once I dropped my pants and put my ass against the stove to burn it but it was just hot, it wasn't hot enough to hurt. So what I did instead was I burned myself with three matches. It was bad. And every time I moved, my jeans rubbed the blisters.

I was just in bed when I heard him coming out of his room downstairs. I heard him peeing. Then I heard a crash. I went down. He hadn't turned on any lights. I turned on the bathroom light. He was sitting up with his back against the wall of the shower. He looked totally out of it. I wondered what he was taking. He looked like my brother Tony after he had been smoking weed. I don't think my dad was into weed. He wasn't cut or anything but there was a broken glass and two toothbrushes on the floor. There was a slight smell of mouthwash.

Are you OK, Dad?

He just looked at me for a minute. Then he said, I never realised it was so much.

What, Dad?

He shook his head. No matter what she says, it wasn't like this from the start.

Dad, you're not making any sense. What are you talking about?

He started to cry. I never thought I would see my dad cry. It was horrible. Then he pulled out about a metre of toilet paper and tore it off and bundled it up and wiped his eyes and blew his nose. He didn't look at me. He was looking down at something on the stone floor. There was a dead woodlouse there that I killed yesterday. I'm scared of woodlice. Now it looked like a dead decepticon. I don't think he was looking at that.

Dad?

I wish my heart finished the job.

First I wasn't sure I heard right. Then I didn't know what to say. It's not a child's job to stop their father wanting to die. Where would I learn that? I tried to think what they told us. Let your friend talk. Seek help from someone you trust. Jesus wept twice. Who even lives out here in this crappy wilderness?

Dad, talk to me.

Now he looked up at me. I smell burning, he said.

There's nothing burning, Dad.

He shrugged. I don't think he could see me properly. He was looking at me like I was hollow.

This country, he said, is never going to last. Will I tell you why, Suzy? Because the odds are always stacked against the little man. Anyone who wants to do anything. The country is full of wasters and scroungers. I'm supposed to pay so they can live like fucking kings. They want to take my money and throw it down their gullets out of pint glasses. The money I earned the hard way? Well, I'll tell you something for nothing, they're not going to get me. Oh no, they're not going to fucking get me.

He got up from the floor.

Dad, I should get a doctor.

He walked past me and out and carefully closed the bathroom door behind him. I opened it again and I was just in time to see him closing his bedroom door. What just happened? Did my dad actually talk to me? Whatever he said, I didn't understand it. Maybe people in my family are talking all the time but I just don't have whatever you need to get it? I heard him getting into the bed. The frame creaks. Then silence. If I waited long enough, if I didn't freeze to death standing there, I would hear him snoring. I waited a while and then I went back into the bathroom and picked up the broken glass. It was the mouthwash. I cleaned the toothbrushes in case there were glass bits. I went to bed. I was shaking.

Like in English we're always supposed to Watch Out For The Turning Point. It's a big deal. But mostly in real life you've already turned. Nobody remembers when there was a signpost or just a crossroads or even any other way. Or even if. And it's just everything is different but also the same in a weird way. Like I wanted to be a doctor when I was in Third Year and I went to this lecture by a guy whose job it was to inject cancer cells into mice. He was saying how you could tag the cells with dye so the tumours would be easy to find. And halfway through the lecture I realised that I already didn't want to be a doctor and that I didn't want to be one for a long time before I came. I couldn't work out when it started. I didn't want to see slides of coloured mouse cancers. I hate mice tbh. But I wouldn't vote to give them cancer if there was a referendum on cancer for mice. Like, I'm. Just. Not. Going. There.

I got out early. I told my teacher I was feeling sick.

But that night was a Turning Point. And I knew it even before I fell asleep. I texted Holly. I think my dad is gonna kill himself. She didn't reply. She was probably asleep. I texted again later. I don't know what to do I'm scared. It was probably one a.m. By two the rain was over and the wind was going down. I dozed off and woke some time later and the wind was gone. I could hear the sea falling on the rocks. I could hear my dad snoring. So I knew he wasn't dead. I fell asleep again.

Next morning I texted my mam. I said where we were and that Dad was depressed and living on sleeping tablets. I said I was worried that he might do something. And my mam texted back: Is that what he told you to say? I said: He didn't tell me to say anything he doesn't know I have my phone he's asleep all the time we have no money its 11 miles to the shop theres only an old guy who sells turf. I didn't care if it was a lie. I just wanted it to stop.

So my mam stayed three days. I don't know why. Every day she hated the place more and I loved it more which was funny because I started out the other way round. Maybe I loved it because she hated it. Now I didn't want to ever go home. I even got to love the noise of the sea. Like you had to think, it spent a billion years trying to tear the land down and never gave up. Bit by bit it's chipping it away. In the end the sea will win.

I used to walk down to Peter's house every morning after breakfast just to get out of their way. We'd have tea and biscuits and he'd tell me stories. Sometimes you could believe his stories while he was telling them and sometimes you could not. But I liked listening to him.

He told me that when he was young he went in the boats. He fished a while with a man who had a boat at the pier below and there were three other men in the boat besides himself and the skipper. One day the son of one of the men called out to him as they were just leaving the pier and the boat had to tie up to the wall again and let the man off and he went home and sent another man in his place because once a man crossed the threshold onto the sea he could not be called from the shore. It was bad luck. It would bring misfortune on the boat to call a man back the same as when a man died you should not call his soul back. The sea was a threshold and death was a threshold and there were others that he could not remember. So that man missed out on that day's fishing because his son wanted him, and he missed out on his share of the catch, because they were paid in shares. Another time a huge beam of wood as big as a herring trawler came ashore just east of his house in the little bay called Cuaisín and there were five strong men on it and they said they were wanting a sixth to manage the beam properly and undertake adventures with them and they called for volunteers, and there was a young man in the village who would risk anything for the pleasure of it and he jumped onto the beam and the six of them set off again out to sea. The young man could see no means of propulsion. There was no engine and no sail and no oar. He thought that it was very strange but he said nothing. And the five men walked about the beam and seemed to be working the ship, but they had nothing to work with and the young man thought it was very strange but he said nothing. But when they were far enough off the shore that the people looked like specks the other five men vanished and their places were taken by five seagulls. It was at that moment the young man realised that the men were sailors lost at sea in some old war and the beam was an enchanted beam. Now, thought the young man, I'm for it as sure as eggs. He looked around him to see was there any way he could take the beam of wood in charge, but there was nothing on it only an old shirt. He thought long and hard and after a time he picked up the shirt and he tied the sleeves to his belt and held the tail of it up. A wind was just after rising and luckily enough it was a wind towards the land for it was a summer's day. He made a sail of the shirt and by walking back and forth along the beam he was able to direct it again towards the shore. The seagulls were not pleased at all and they first of all made a terrible racket, and then when they saw what he was at they started to attack him. But this young lad was a mighty dancer and they could no more catch him than Sonny Liston could catch Cassius Clay. By and by he brought the beam ashore and the seagulls flew away and the people took the beam and found that it was the very best of wood from South America, a kind of mahogany that they call ironwood. They turned it into keels and keelsons and king planks and ribs for their boats and it was always said that a boat out of Cuaisín would never drown. That man's name was Patrick Leahy and he was an old man when I was a boy.

They were the kind of stories that Peter told me. Tbh I think he never learned about the realistic convention in Leaving Cert. Like we almost didn't do it ourselves except someone found out about it on Wikipedia. It was like he lived in a fairy story himself idk here he was on his own miles from anywhere and his head was full of these things. It was sad. Somebody should write them all down before he dies.

Why didn't you marry someone, Peter?

I was never taken enough with anyone, he said. The girls around here are flighty and I never liked flightiness.

I didn't know what flightiness meant, but I thought maybe it could mean someone like Serena and I could see why he wouldn't want to marry someone like that. And then again maybe I was flighty myself idk. I was going to say I didn't like flighty girls either but I thought I might give the wrong impression. So instead I told him about Holly and he said I was lucky to have such a good friend. I told him that my family was totally dysfunctional, if you google it we have nearly all the signs, and I didn't know which of them I'd kill first, my dad or my mam. He thought that was funny. Oh kill your father, he said. Fathers is always trouble, although it's nearly always the son kills the father, still they could make an exception once in a while. The two of us chuckled about that. I said only for Holly I would go crackers. He went and made another pot of tea. We had scoffed all the biscuits by then. I could hear him whistling through his teeth in the kitchen. It is the lonesomest sound. Or so I believe anyway.

But my dad got no sleeping pills all the time she was here. She got him up every day and they went on walks. Sometimes I had to go with them but sometimes not. The first day he could only walk a few hundred metres. I googled sleeping pills but they never said anything about weakness. I started to see things about motor neurone disease and multiple sclerosis. Like maybe he had what Stephen Hawking had? But Stephen Hawking is a genius. If you google anything medical you get a million hits for whatever is the worst nightmare of your life. But the second day he could walk further, and on the third day we all walked out to the point together. I decided he didn't have motor neurone disease. And Peter came up to see how we were getting on and my mam sent him into the village with a list and he came back with fruit and chocolate biscuits and frozen pizzas and stuff. I realised I should have bought frozen pizzas when I was shopping. It would have been a lot easier and I wouldn't have eaten three quarters of a sheep while my dad was asleep.

There was no fighting. Dinner was more like at Serena's. The only bit of hassle took place when Mam told him that Dan Kelleher got the nomination while he was away. My dad said, Are you trying to twist the knife in the wound?

I'm just saying.

Well you didn't have to fucking say it.

Well, if you were at home you might have stopped him.

My dad shrugged. That fucker is like a rat. He can weasel his way into anything. There's no stopping a cunt like that.

My mother said, Mind your language in front of Suzy.

Dad looked at me. Suzy has her own language.

Then on the third afternoon, the day we all walked up to the point, my mam said, Ok, Matt, you're back on your feet now, time for me to go home. And my dad said, Thanks. And my mam said, You had your little drama, come back when you find the guts to face it, but I'm taking Suzy with me.

I couldn't believe it. She was leaving. I thought they were sorted. And I knew if I left Dad here he would stop eating again. He would die. Or he would jump into the sea.

Get your things and get into the car, Suzy.

I shook my head. No, Mam.

Get into the car now.

No, Mam. I can't.

She looked at me and then she looked at my dad. I looked at him too and I saw he was smiling. Like a little smile. Like he was doing his best to hide it but he couldn't. My mam got into the car and drove away. We watched her as long as we could. We could see the roof of the car winking in the sunlight away down towards Peter's house. Then it was gone.

OK, my dad said, that didn't work. Plan B.

I stared at him. Like what didn't work? He's lying in the bed dying and it's Plan B? He went into the house and after approximately thirty seconds I could hear him on his phone. The phone he told me was in a bin at the office. Now I really wanted to run down through the field and take a flier over the edge. I even turned round and tried to figure out a way to get over the barbed wire without ripping my jeans until I realised that ripped jeans wouldn't matter so much if I threw myself in the sea. Then my dad came out. He pressed the button that opened the car and the lights flashed. It makes a little squeaking sound. A sheep that was eating something on a ditch looked around. She didn't give a flying fuck. We could drive into the sea and she would still be eating grass.

Get your kit, Suzy, we're moving out.

I didn't know if he was happy or just decisive. He was businesslike. This was how he bought houses. He already had a plan. In his mind there are plans and mostly they work. In my life plans are all fucked up. There is no plan because everything just happens. I am always at the fall-back position and still falling.

The white road home. Even the bogs were bleached white by winter. Some kind of bleached reeds or long grass maybe and these crazy walls whitened by lichen. To make the fields they had to take the stones out first otherwise they would have been stone fields. Nobody grows stones. Sometimes the field was so small you could hardly stand in it. And in places there were the scabs of cut turf and the scar of the cutaway. We drove home through the mountains and came out in a place where there were buses and houses and small towns with WiFi cafes and I knew then we were going to finish up at home and everything would start all over again. This must be some kind of hell, where all your mistakes keep happening no matter what you do.

And after about an hour my dad rang someone and found out that Kelleher was spreading rumours that my dad was in trouble with the Revenue, and Great-To-Meet Micky Molloy told Somebody Somebody that his relationship with my dad was purely on a business footing. My dad said he would sue Dan Kelleher. Like, what was the story there? My dad was going to be bankrupted by the Revenue and he was going to sue Dan Kelleher, future member of parliament for the Blue Party once Great-To-Meet Micky retired? Like me and Holly did a project once for Civics. The most common jobs our public representatives had before they were elected was teachers, auctioneers, salesmen and farmers. Some of them did two of the jobs. Farmer and auctioneer. So Dan Kelleher was as good as in the door. All he needed was someone to die, preferably Micky, and there would be a by-election. Or maybe we were due a general election. They're meant to change every five years but as far as I can see it's always the same people anyway. Teachers, auctioneers, salesmen, farmers. It's meant to be democracy. Idk.

The other thing he found out was that Bowles was replacing the gates at Ballyshane. They were iron gates. My dad said they were there since famine times. He couldn't believe it. This English cunt coming over here and throwing our gates out. But, Dad, I said, Miss Corry let them rust away.

Never mind what Miss Corry did. She was one of our own.

Seriously, Dad, I said, like the Corrys?

No way, my dad said, should he be allowed to touch those gates. Those gates are part of our history.

Like the gates were part of our history all right. They were closed on the famine. They got the starving humble peasants to build a nice limestone wall around them and they Paid Them In Soup. That was the Furneys of course, and the Corrys bought the estate from them, but still the Corrys were huntingshootingfishing and they

205

didn't exactly tear the wall down after the revolution. Even Miss Corry wore a tweed suit. Idk. They were just different. They might as well have been Protestant. Leary our History teacher says Catholic landlords were as bad or worse than Protestant landlords. A landlord is a landlord, Leary says. Holly's dad says my dad is suffering from false consciousness. I said I thought he was suffering from depression or psychosis or something. She says he's a bourgeois. Can't deny that. At least he's a wannabe bourgeois. If he could be a Corry he would be. Matt Corry–Regan would suit him fine. Or Regan–Corry. But my dad doesn't have the class to be a proper bourgeois. He just makes money and joins clubs. Clubs never turn money away. And if they did my dad would build a terrace of houses on the fifth green or whatever. He'd get planning for it too. My dad always gets what he wants.

And I found out that Serena had a date. Like, Hi suzy i got a date with my master satrdy at 3.

Fuck my life, Jesus, I swear I don't know how I live through it.

And when we turned in the gate the trees were in flower. Like the only trees in my garden are mountain ash, because they remind my mam of her place, where her people came from, which is mountainy. But I had my window open and the car filled with the smell of sex idk whatever the mountain ash flowers smell like it just reminds me of sex, I'm not going to explain, just think about it. It was sad.

Naturally there was no Plan B. There never is. B stands for bullshit. All we did was arrive during the day when the house was empty and put our things in the washing machine.

That was my idea. I couldn't wait to get a wash going. By that time I was wearing Vintage Pre-Worn Panties.

When my mam came home we were already there. She took one look at us and put a frozen pizza in the oven.

I assume you looked after yourselves, she said.

Dad said we had chicken and chips on the way home.

There was no fight. There was no talk of a summons idk maybe my dad was just making stuff up. Maybe it was all about my mam. The way things are in my house I'm never going to find out. But it's like when you have a fight in school and you walk away and you're hoping the other person idk maybe a Serena-like individual will call after you, Come back, Suzy, all is forgiven. But there's already too much to forgive and nobody is ever going to call. But like I need someone to call. Maybe more than my dad, I need it.

I never slept a wink even though I was in my own bed again. I couldn't stop waiting. The Macbeths slept like kings until they murdered someone, like uneasy lies the head idk but I got sleeplessness for even just thinking about it, or even like just worrying that something might happen. But nothing did. It's just they went to bed. Tony came home about two. Maybe I dozed off idk about five o'clock I heard a fox barking somewhere. It was a she-fox maybe, a sound like a woman screaming, a short hard scream. I hear it often around my house at night. We are miles from anywhere.

So next day I went to school and Holly and Serena wanted to know all about it. I told them about Peter. Serena said, Like, you found this old depressed guy in a bog somewhere, that is so you, Suzy, just totally gross, he was probably a gay.

But Holly understood. When I think of it now Peter was Holly. He was that thing which is just gentleness. Which I need. Someone to be with where I don't have to run or hide. I was lucky I found him. He maybe saved me. And Holly was still saying no to Jason Clancy. She showed me one of his texts. Babe u gotta let me xplain im not an asshole I just say de rong tings ☹.

Like, rong? How could anyone spell it like that?

I said, Tell him to try autocorrect.

She didn't get it.

He was even tweeting her. Holly said he was practically stalking her. She was trying to block his number but you can only block calls on her phone.

And all Serena wanted to talk about was the Graham Dwyer trial. She knew all about it and she had googled all the things they did.

Holly was like, Too much information Serena, I don't need to know this. And we're in school. So Serena

209

decided to tell Holly the whole story. It's a kind of BDSM thing is how I figure it, forcing other people to hear things they don't want, especially about sex. Or like toilet or something. She was like: This guy who arranged with a girl to stab her to death during sex (breathlessly). She suffered from death wish, you know? And he did it, like totally stabbed her to death (eyes widen in pretend shock). I don't know if he had sex with her because they only found her bones so like duh no forensics (grin). The guy was married with kids but he had this secret life (eyes open again and she looked at me). And they did bondage and they had all these brilliant bondage objects, like a ball gag and handcuffs and (whisper) an anal plug.

Like Serena actually said anal plug in my school!!?? Even if it was a whisper. Serena does not really do whisper.

So what about the dead girl Suzy found?

Way! I only found the purse!

Serena was big eyed. You're right, she said, what if it's the same thing?

This was rape and murder, I said. The woman didn't like make contact with a possible euthaniser or whatever. Is that even a word?

Serena ignored me. It was like this deliberate ignore, like you see.

Dwyer buried the woman someplace and threw all her things into a lake and during a dry summer people found stuff. Phones idk stuff (gesture of raising empty hands). It was like some film. And at the same time a completely freaky accident (eyes open wide again), a dog walker found her bones, well the dog found her bones, you know dogs and bones? Like a human skeleton is bone heaven for a dog (she doesn't bat an eyelid). Like it was the perfect crime because the girl was suicidal and it shouldn't be a crime at all because the girl wanted to die.

And I kept saying, It's too sad, it's too sad. I wanted her to stop telling us about it now.

He'll get life, Serena said, and all he did was help her.

Holly took two steps back and looked at her. For fuck's sake, Serena, are you even for real?

Then she walked away. Which left Serena and me alone. Well, not alone because we were in the hall and the place was full af with girls and random teachers. But I was afraid she'd ask me what I thought. So I said, I don't know what I'm going to say to Leary, I never got my essay done.

Then the bell went.

My teachers gave me hell of course. This is your Leaving Cert Year, Suzy Regan, you're never going to get an A if you don't shape up.

That kind of shit. It's their job.

But Leary just shook his head and started on revising the Battle of Stalingrad. It's like he understands.

The big news was that Serena had an actual not Jason, not Larrydemaster, boyfriend. Holly told me. I don't know if you can believe that. Terms and conditions apply with Serena. I said that to Holly but she said no she was legit dating this guy from the Brothers'. What Holly was amazed about was that he was meant to be a nice guy. Or so people said. What's a nice guy doing with Serena The Hate Message Queen? His name was Jack. It wasn't James or John, it was Jack from the start. Like we both knew Serena was doomed to end up with some sleazeball, but Holly was saying this Jack was OK. It was a miracle. He was a year younger than Serena. He was in fifth year in the Brothers'. He was in the Brothers' and we were in the Nuns' and there were no Brothers in his place and no Nuns in ours. All the brothers and nuns evacuated the premises before we arrived. But we were still coming down with religion. I asked Holly if Serena had done anything with him yet and she said she didn't think so, they went to the pictures and they went to a food place and that was all. She heard they went to see *Minions,* which is just totally Serena. A film about depressed unmotivated single-cell organism descendants who live in a cave is as good as Michelangelo to her. Or Da Vinci or whatever. Somebody big. I saw the trailer and it looks like crap.

What's not generally known is that my grandad practically disowned my dad. This was because my dad wanted to sell my grandad's farm. He didn't just want to sell it, he wanted to develop it. He wanted to build forty unique luxury executive-style residences each to a different design and standing on between half an acre and three quarters with pre-landscaped gardens. My grandad's farm was eleven acres. Eleven point seven to be precise. It was all he ever owned, that and the house he lived in. My dad announced his plan. My grandad would sign over the land to his son for love and affection. That is the legal term. My dad would develop the land, which he insisted on calling the site, and set aside one house for my grandad. That was his first mistake. My granny died in my grandad's house. He didn't want to move into an executive-style residence. You never saw anybody less like an executive than my grandad. He made his living growing vegetables, keeping pigs and a few cattle. When the tax relief for horses came in he bought a mare and bred foals. His back was bad idk like what happens to people's backs? He used to say, Suzy my back is destroyed. When he stood up he would take five minutes holding his back and forcing himself to straighten bit by bit. That's how I remember him – his hand on his back, straightening slowly like a branch that was bent for a long time. So my dad laid out his commercial proposition and my grandad listened and then he said, The best you can do now, Matt Regan, is bugger off home before I go upstairs and get the shotgun, for I'd just as soon shoot the arse off you as listen to you.

My dad made a second mistake. He thought my grandad was joking.

So my grandad went upstairs and came down with the shotgun with two number five cartridges in his hand.

My dad left.

What my grandad did was change his will to leave the farm to my mam. My mam wouldn't sell it so we still own it even though we sold the house. She was crazy about my grandad. He used to call her girl, even after she had me when no way was she a girl. Sometimes when I want to just walk away I go there. Someone else is renting the land from us. He keeps cattle on it. That's why it's called Regan's Glen. We sold the house and it's gone now. The dude who bought it bulldozed the dwelling house and outhouses and then ran out of money. I think his plan was to build a unique luxury executive-style residence. It's what we all aspire to in Ireland. But he ended up emigrating to Qatar where he works on building hotels for people who would rather be somewhere nice.

My grandad used to say, Suzy, girl, the land is for you. Even if you have only an acre you have something.

He tried to persuade me to keep pigs. Me. A pig would eat you, they are vicious bastards. I googled it. I could just see myself getting knocked over and looking up at a pig who wanted the full Irish for his breakfast. Remember, I even thought about having pigs eat my mam during my axe-murder phase.

So now when my mam is pissed with me she says, You better go and buy a pig because I'm not keeping you a minute more in this house.

And maybe I will buy a pig. Maybe I could train him to talk like in that film. It was OK. I saw it on telly. Some people stopped eating pork chops afterwards. Like I would.

Maybe he would like me and not want to eat me. And we could have a pet and mistress relationship. Not. Definitely not like *Fifty Shades of Grey*. Not even Two Shades of It.

And one thing that everybody knows is that my dad has like fourteen of the fifteen personality traits of the psychopath. And he's working on the last one.

So they picked Bowles up for questioning about the murder. That was a surprise. Like I said to Dad, He's gay, he wouldn't do it. Dad was unaware of the gayness thing. He didn't believe it. I also pointed out that he was smaller than me, like no way could he overpower a fit young woman. My dad said he could have been one of the violent gays and they get amazing strength. So then we had a conversation about the violent gays which I was unaware of as a specific type of gay. My dad said it was well known and that was that. When my dad thinks something is well known it usually means he made it up or it's some crap he heard on a talk show.

He came up to my room that night to tell me that he thought if Bowles was convicted of murder Ballyshane might come up for sale again. I said I wouldn't hold my breath. He said a certain friend of his in the guards (the 'a certain' was a bit unnecessary as he only knows one guard) also told him that Bowles was an object of suspicion anyway for some reason.

And what you said about him being a gay? I mean, would he be the woman-hater type? Sometimes gays take it out on women, for being like, gay, you know, for rejecting them or something.

I rolled my eyes.

Dad, I said, I don't think it's actually like that for gays. I mean I think they're just gay, you know. And I don't know what type he is. I didn't know there were types. All I know is he's gay. I don't think gays rape women all that much. Like when did you last hear of a woman being raped and murdered by a gay man? It's just not their thing. The people who rape and murder women are straight men.

We don't know that. You'd have to be twisted to rape and murder someone, right?

Yeah but twisted and gay are two different things, Dad. And I'm pretty sure the *Sunday Independent* would be all over a story about a gay man going around raping women. And *The Sun*. Front page stuff.

I could see him thinking it over. He reads the *Independent*.

OK, well goodnight, Suzy.

Goodnight, Dad.

He closed the door then opened it again. If you hear anything more about your man Bowles let me know.

I will, Dad.

Then before I got to sleep my mam came up. She sat on my bed. It was like when I was small. Suzy, she said, you were right to text me that time, you did the right thing, you were looking after your dad.

Mam, are you and Dad going to split up?

I don't know, pet. We're in a lot of trouble right now. But your dad will make it. You can't keep him down forever. He's a fighter.

I was going to say, Tony is a fighter too by the looks of it but mostly he gets hammered.

But I didn't. And my mam said goodnight and I said goodnight and then she went to bed herself. Tonight was a world record for goodnights. Something must be happening. There was something just perf about it. Then I thought, How sad am I, one night my mam and dad say goodnight to me and I tear up like someone proposed to me? I'm pathetic. But I was happy falling asleep. I don't know, sometimes things get better. Maybe.

I'm like at my bus stop on my way to school reading a long text from Serena when Tom Bowles' car stops beside me. Tom Bowles gets out. I am seriously scared. He is a Murder Suspect. I get my phone out and start to think who to phone, like not Serena, and Holly will be here any minute, and not my mam and not my dad because he wouldn't have a clue. And not the guards because I would have to confess about the bin. But Tom Bowles doesn't attack me. He says, Hello, Miss. It's Suzy isn't it?

Hiya.

Do you remember me?

Yeah, you're the Ballyshane guy.

Is that how you say it? I thought it was pronounced Ballyshane.

No it's shaan, like there's a fada on the a. Like bane field, you know. I don't know, it's how we say Irish names around here. It's different. It's not English English.

I knew I should shut up.

Could I ask you a favour?

There's no harm in asking. I might not do it though.

That's perfectly fine. I'm sure you know that the police brought me in for questioning about that terrible murder.

I nodded. I didn't know what to say. What Do You Say To A Murder Suspect?

Well, the thing is I didn't do it and I have an alibi. Unfortunately, for reasons which I will reveal to you shortly, I didn't want to use my alibi. It was just a fishing expedition this time. If it had been more serious I would have had to use it. But I get the feeling they don't like me and they would like nothing better than to set me up. Do you catch my drift?

My bus is coming.

I think you should miss your bus.

I can't I'll be late for school.

I'll drive you in.

No thanks. Here's the bus now and here's my friend Holly.

It's about the night you set fire to my bin.

Oh.

I stayed where I was. Holly came running with her bag bouncing on her back. She shouted to me as she got on. She was in such a hurry she didn't notice that I was staying. Then the bus pulled off and I saw Holly's face glued to the glass watching us. Then Thirty Other Faces Turned Too. All these people looking at me. It felt like I was being left behind in some extermination camp or a ghetto. Like you see. The one who's left behind gets sent to the gas chamber. I don't know, maybe I'm making that up. Was it ever a film?

Hop in, my dear, Tom Bowles said. I'll drive you to school.

It's like this, he said, as he pulled out onto the road. The police believe the murder was committed the night you and your friend set fire to my bin. They have CCTV footage of the young lady getting into a car outside a public house at about midnight, and they believe she was killed some time after that, probably around four a.m. because her watch was broken when she was thrown into the valley.

I found her purse, I said.

Really? I didn't know that.

Well The Dog found it. I reported it.

Dogs do often find bodies. It happens a lot. You know, The body was found by a man out walking his dog. You hear that a lot. It must have been horrible for you.

It was kind of exciting I don't know. I just thought it was a purse but I got suspicious because there was money still in it. I reported it.

Well, my little problem is this. If I tell the police about the bin they will ask me to prove that I'm telling the truth. Now as it happens we have proof positive. Do you get my drift? The proof is your good self.

My mam will kill me. And Serena's dad will throw her out. He's a fucking freak you have no idea. We call him Willy The Right To Life. He's a mad pro-lifer. Like his hands were blessed by the Pope.

Tom Bowles was chuckling. Your brother mentioned him. I wondered who he was.

My brother?

So if I call the police up and say I've just remembered something that happened that night, will you talk to them?

But my dad will like totally kill me. My mam will slaughter me. I can't do it. This is my school here.

We pulled over beside the school gate. He didn't drive in. I don't know what Serena would have said if she saw me getting out of Tom Bowles' car. Holly wouldn't say anything. The bell was gone I could see. Everybody was going in. For the first time in my life I wanted to be in school.

Well, we can do it two ways. I can name you and they will call to your house to check it, or you can volunteer and I'll say you've promised to come into the station to give them a statement. Once I'm eliminated from their enquiries they won't be interested in you any more. They'll want your friend too. You should both go in. Grace will drive you if you like. She likes police officers.

Grace likes police officers?

She has a thing for strong men, our Grace.

I have to go, the bell is gone.

My card, he said, handing me his card like they do in detective stories. Call me tonight or else I'll go ahead. I need to let them know tomorrow at the latest.

How do you like Ballyshane? I asked as I got out.

I like it, he said, it's just the kind of place I like. Homely.

My dad is hoping you get charged with the murder and he'll buy the house when you get thrown in gaol.

I closed the door and walked away. I saw that Holly was waiting for me at the student door. I knew I had to tell her everything. She would know what to do. But I couldn't tell her about Serena's message in which she explained in about two hundred words and twenty texts how she was meeting the master dude, the guy from alt.com, he was totally cool, had loads of toys, she wanted me to go with her. To have her back. Like you do.

I replied: I don't believe a word of it n if it's true I'm not going.

Serena: Bitch I own you.

At small break we had a conversation. Holly said the guards were probably just Checking Out Possible Leads. They needed to Eliminate Him From Enquiries. If I could give him an alibi he would be in the clear and the guards would forget about it. We both knew we were really taking part in an episode of *Rebus*. We could talk the talk. They should take us on as scriptwriters. But like we also knew simultaneously that it was total bullshit. It's just that bullshit has a way of getting you to do things. That's why all those generals made speeches before battle. Napoleon and Richard III and that British guy who was going to Iraq, the famous leader type. Because bullshit makes you fight. But we decided we should do it. I was to text Tom Bowles. So we went and got Serena and explained to her how it was going to be, and she was like, Cool, cool, my dad will murder me but cool by me. She looked stoned. Holly said it was love. Serena had a bag full of samples from some cosmetic company. She watches out for special offers online. She was sharing it out. She had Crème Hyaluronique for filling deep wrinkles, a Traceur Hyaluronique Comblement for precise wrinkles, a Crème Silicium Regard for a lifting effect, a Crème Bio-Protectrice for sensitive or reactive skin, a Masque

Bio-Apaisant Immédiat for soothing sensitive or reactive skin, a Serum Bio-Reparateur for repairing sensitive or reactive skin, and factor fifty suntan lotion. For about an hour she was at peak popularity in my school. Holly and me don't use.

And after school we went into town instead of getting the bus and we Presented Ourselves At The Station ^—^. The station was not anything like on telly. You walked in the door of this crappy building and there was a big counter like a post office, and a noticeboard with posters about Firearms Licences and Help Numbers and A Missing Dog, and behind the counter there was a Huge Map and two scabby filing cabinets. And There Was No One There. On telly there's always people moving around and slagging each other off. We pressed a button and we heard a buzzer somewhere else and after a few minutes a small fat man in a uniform came out.

What can I do for you kids?

Kids, Serena said, we're like fucking seniors in our school. In six months we'll be in university.

He winked at her. But Policemen Never Wink.

Don't be using language now. It's unbecoming in a lady.

I said, We want to confess.

He smiled. Now what have you to confess?

We did something, Serena said. Aren't you supposed to tell us we don't have to say anything but anything we do say may be taken down and used against us in a court of law?

Yeah, I said, we're entitled to be cautioned. It's a human right.

Don't believe everything you see on TV, he said.

Do you want to hear our confession or not?

Fire away so girls. In your own good time. In nominy patry et filiy et spirity sancty amen. He made the sign of the cross at us and winked. How long is it since your last confession, ladies?

I said, I feel your pain. But I'm an atheist.

He just looked at me. I looked at him. I was thinking, ffs if this is the standard of the justice system. Guards are knobheads.

He picked up a pen but I noticed he didn't write anything down. Like two girls must walk into his station every day and confess to something. It wasn't until we mentioned the date and Ballyshane that he woke up. He told us to sit down for a minute. There was someone would want to talk to us. He came back with a man. The man had a different accent, like maybe Dublin.

I'm thinking, This is more like it.

After that we were brought into a room and sat at a table exactly like on telly and the man and a woman guard came in and that was where we made our statements. I did the talking except every now and then I'd say, Right, Serena? And Serena would say, Right. In the middle, it was so embarrassing, my brother's phone ass-called me and I was like, Hello? Hello? Tony your phone is ass-calling me? Then I hung up and it called again. The guard asked me to turn it off. The woman guard wrote everything down. Maybe she even wrote down that I was ass-called twice. Every now and then she stopped and asked me to repeat something or slow down. The man asked the questions. When I got to the light coming on and I said I saw Tom Bowles and the housekeeper, he stopped me.

Do you know that or do you believe it?

That was an interesting question. I said I knew it and I believed it. But I said I supposed you could believe something and not know it, or you could know something and not believe it. Like once I remember I crushed a glass in my hand and cut myself and I said, I don't fucking believe this. And I didn't believe it for like three seconds.

That's enough, the man said. Just carry on.

So then I got to legging it and getting home. I didn't mention that Serena wasn't with me. And I told them how my dad and mam were awake because of the alarm going off and how they nearly gutted me. And the man said to the woman guard, We could check with the alarm company.

Then they checked on things like What Were Our Names And Addresses, Were We Sure About The Time and What We Observed and Whether We Were Sure About Seeing Mr Bowles?

And then they asked us why did we set fire to the Ballyshane recycling bin and I just couldn't think of an answer. And after a few seconds I realised Serena was pointing at me. And then she said, still pointing at me, It was her idea, she's like a pyromaniac. And I said that was a lie. And Serena said, Cross my heart and swear to die it was Suzy's idea. And I said, I don't fucking believe this. And after a few more rounds of that the guards told us just sign the statements and get lost.

We signed. I don't know about Serena but I felt like a character in *Cracker* or *Rebus*. It was fab. Like even being a character who was sold out by her best friend. Or one of her friends anyway. It was still fab. Holly was going to be mad jealous.

Then, just like Colombo, before I went out the door I said, Oh by the way, the housekeeper? He's a cross-dresser.

And then I was gone.

But not before I caught the stupid look on the guards' faces. Like they never twigged it. Guards are thick.

Holly was waiting outside. How did it go?

I'm like: She blamed me.

I pointed at Serena.

Serena goes: You said I could.

And I goes: I didn't think you were fucking serious.

Jesus, Serena, Holly goes, giving Serena the bitch stare.

Serena was already on her phone. In maybe three seconds she was talking to Jack. You're not going to believe where I am, Jack... She looked at us and pointed at the phone and then turned her back on us.

Holly said, I don't believe she did that. She's legit a total skanger. I just don't believe it.

They believed us anyhow, I said. I think they did. Maybe.

Holly said they had to believe us because why else would two girls confess to doing damage and practically breaking and entering? I high-fived her. Did you hear the one about the serial killer? He was a fan of The Police.

Holly laughed.

Serena gave us the scan. I could see she hadn't a clue.

Like, The Police, I said, the band, you know?

And at that moment, for no good reason, I suddenly started to wonder where Serena was between the time when we ran away and the time she got back to my house. What was she doing? And then that made me remember that Tom Bowles mentioned Tony. But how did he know my brother? And after that it was bad. I started to cry. I know I did. Like it is just embarrassing how often I cry. And Holly got me onto the bus and got me off at our home stop. I don't remember what happened in between except I remember shaking and feeling cold all over and telling Holly that I was worried about Tony. And I was sad about Peter. Like I missed him. I could do with one of his stories. But really it was all about my dad who is Falling Apart idk like seriously falling apart. I don't know what happened to Serena but that night I got another set of pregnancy texts from her so I suppose herself and Jack must have found someplace to go. But at least this time it sounded like Jack was going to stick around. After the third text I just replied, I can't believe you just blamed me to the guards. And she was like: I pannecked im sorry dont leave me i need u ☹. Then around two o'clock I got a text from her that said, we did it 3 times ☺ i love him so much u have 2 meet him.

Holly had a thing from Facebook. Or maybe Twitter idk.

Best year?

Worst year?

Favourite food?

You added up the last two numbers in each year and the total told you how old you would be when you get married. And then you took the two numbers in the age and picked out the corresponding letters in the favourite food and they were the initials of the person you would marry. Mine was

2013

2015

Omelette

28

M.E.

Holly thought it was hilarious but I thought it was sad because it was probably true. Wait, I said, what if my favourite food was sushi? She said you just kept counting until you got the numbers. So sushi would be SS. I said, that's worse. SS equals Serena Sheils. Oh Jesus, I said, I think I'd rather buy a pig. We just like totally cracked up. We were on the bus and people turned around to see if we were all

231

right. Holly started to do her Ed Sheeran imitation. Holly has Ed Sheeran nailed.

When we calmed down Holly said, Why 2012?

That was my grandad's seventy-fifth.

She squeezed my arm. I remember, she said.

Then I said, What if I had to ask Willy The Right To Life for his daughter's hand in marriage? I'd have to go down on one knee.

And Holly goes: I wouldn't kneel down in front of Willy if you paid me a million.

What would the Pope do?

And that started us off again. We were Rolling On The Floor Laughing. Like virtually literally. I wasn't talking to Serena since the episode in the station when she sold me out so we could laugh at her as much as we liked.

I said, And knowing Serena I'd get a text from her in the middle of the wedding night to say she had to be pregnant because we didn't use anything.

And Holly said, That reminds me. Maura O'Keefe told me Serena was asking her about missing periods.

Oh Jesus.

I know. I forgot to tell you. It was at big break.

Like the night of the cop station she texted me. She said they did it three times.

Me and Holly looked at each other. I don't know what it did to Holly but it made me feel weak all over. Three times. In one night. Well, in one evening, because she would have been home before late. And I was a bit jealous too tbh if she was pregnant. I don't know why that would be. But the thought of a baby growing inside. Like I remember this baby homecoming video and the mother had two scotties and they had the scotties on the bed and the baby cradle thingy and it was just cute. And the scotties liked the baby. Or at least they didn't bite him. They didn't lick him or anything just sort of looked.

Well, Holly said, I'm not going to marry until I'm seventy-eight and his initials are TT.

He'll be a twenty-one-year-old stud toyboy who's marrying you for your money. What was your favourite food?

Spaghetti.

We thought that was hilarious too. We were still laughing when the bus stopped and a boy got on and Holly nudged me in the ribs and whispered, Jack.

He was tall and cool. He had sandy blond hair and blue eyes. He walked past us and for no reason I said, Hi, I'm Suzy. We're friends of Serena.

I didn't tell him that Serena was meeting a man who was into rape bondage and humiliation. If you could believe it. Which frankly I don't. But somehow I felt that if I did tell him he would have understood.

He stopped and said Hi. Then he sat in the empty seat on the other side of the aisle.

So you're Suzy, he said.

And I'm Holly, Holly said, leaning forward so he could see her better.

Hi, Holly.

How's Serena? I said.

She's all right. Like I didn't see her for a week.

We watched the road for a bit. Holly didn't say anything. I was thinking what happened to the three times a night job? The driver had the radio on and they were playing some old country stuff all about how Dolly Parton wanted Jolene not to take her man and shit. Holly couldn't stop her leg from tapping though. I elbowed her. Like no way are any of my friends going to sing along to Dolly Parton. She told me her latest urban legend. A friend of the family had an overheating engine. This happens to friends of Holly's family because they drive crap cars that are past their sell-by date. Their cat liked to sleep on the engine at night. But one day they noticed the cat was missing. After about a week they noticed there was always a smell of cooking when they were driving. We thought that was funny. And after a bit Jack leaned across the aisle and said, They play some desperate shite on this bus. Holly and me laughed but I was thinking like what bus does he usually get and do they play good stuff on his one? Eventually I thought of something else to say.

Serena texted me about you. She said I should meet you. She thinks you're fab.

Holly giggled. I was a bit annoyed that she was giggling but I couldn't do anything about it.

Cool, he said, Want to leave me your mobile?

So I gave him my number and he gave me his and we put them in our phones and named them and by then our stop was coming up. And then we had each other in our contacts. And idk it was kind of exciting and naughty idk. But I wanted to ask something and just after I pressed the stop bell I said, So are you still seeing her?

I am yeah, kind of.

That's cool so. This is my stop.

And afterwards Holly said, So what's the story, Suzy? What was that about?

I said I was curious because Serena makes stuff up, like telling stories. You can never trust a word that comes out of her mouth. Look at the time she told the guards burning the bin was my idea. And how are we to know she does all that shit? Like if she actually turned out to be pregnant we'd know QED but until then we don't have a clue. She could be a compulsive liar. I googled that and it turned up a lot of interesting stuff. Like compulsive liars tell people things to make themselves important. They dream up whole stories about their lives, sometimes they even live two lives. It begins with a sense of inferiority and a feeling of worthlessness. And she has worthlessness in spades. Look at how she was cutting and the time she overdosed. Like she fits everything, a hundred per cent. But Holly said once you start googling stuff it's easy to fit it, it's like a horoscope in a magazine, even if you read the wrong one by mistake you think it could be you. If you have something wrong with you, like bad period pains, and you google it, it turns out you have whatever is the worst possible thing you could have.

I didn't want to say so, but I actually did google extreme pain in lower stomach a week before and I turned up ovarian cancer and I was so scared I actually turned my phone off. Like I haven't deliberately turned my phone off in over a year. Can you imagine what it feels like to have your phone actually off permanently for a period of hours? My grandad had lung cancer but it was the secondary cancer that killed him. It was in his head. He died on a trolley in Accident and Emergency because they couldn't find a bed for him. Even though the Minister For Health said that waiting lists had been eliminated. Even though he was pretty far gone and inclined to fall over even if he sat up, he was able to tell my mam that the trolley situation was a fucking disgrace and the best thing to do was to put the whole government up against a wall and shoot them. My grandad came from a generation where they would do that too. I miss him.

In a way The Crash killed him, like the Economic Crash. Not straight off. It was a sort of a hit at an obtuse angle. A glancing blow, like you see. They ran out of doctors and nurses. My grandad didn't have Private, even though my mam said she'd pay for it. My dad wouldn't pay for it because of Grandad changing his will. Fair is fair, he said when my mam suggested it. You have to hand it to my dad, he can carry a grudge.

Holly says put a hot water bottle on your period and it does help, but sometimes I get a headache with it and two hot water bottles is just gross. But my guess is that Holly googled it too. How many girls in the world all googling period pains and getting hits for ovarian cancer? Who needs horror movies when we have our phones?

That night he texted me. It was about ten o'clock. I was in bed doing Physics. Like, I can do Physics because I remember the entire textbook. If they ever ask me something that's not in *Real World Physics* I'm a goner. The diagram shows a ray of light travelling from glass to air. The ray of light undergoes refraction at B. And then my phone bings. Like it was just: Sup Suzy, what r u up 2? And I just replied: Doing physics. But it made me happy, I don't know why. And so after about an hour, when I was just turning over to Maths I texted him: How's it going? And he said: Cool. I liked talking on d bus today. And that started me thinking, What was he doing on our bus? I didn't ask him though. Instead I texted Holly that Jack texted me. Woah girl, she said, wat r u up 2? I said I didn't know, I was just starting Maths. Then she texted me: Whats de Moivre's theorem? Like you can tell someone something like that in text. I said I'd explain it tomorrow. But just for the laugh anyway I texted her (Cos A + iSin A)n = Cos nA + iSin nA ☺. It took me about twenty minutes to work out how to do it on my phone. And she went: Help ☹!!!! I told her I'd go over it on the bus tomorrow morning and she

237

could come to my house and I'd give her a full grind on Wednesday half-day when my mam wouldn't be home. Like I have de Moivre's Theorem nailed. Every night last thing Holly and me text each other. The first one always says: Goodnight sleep tight. And the other replies: Don't let the bugs bite ☺. So I was in the bathroom getting ready when a text came in. I took no notice. I was in the shower but I heard it. Then a second text came in. That was strange. I dried myself off and got into my pjs and took the phone to bed. The first text said: Wanna meet me after school? Maybe do sumthng? It was from Jack. The second one said: Goodnight sleep tight. I replied to the second one first. I said Don't let the bugs bite ☺. Then I replied to the first one. Yes.

Then I thought WTF AM I LOSING IT??? If Serena finds out she will never forgive me. Like she will Kill Herself Properly. But then Friday was midterm break and Serena and her mother were going to visit her auntie who had something wrong with her. They always went February midterm. And I needn't tell Holly anything. Holly is one of life's innocents. I sent Jack another text: Saturday? And he said: Perf I'll pick u up ill have my Moms car.

And that night my brother came home earlier than usual. I was still awake. I was too nervous to sleep. When I heard him in the kitchen I went downstairs. He was sitting at the kitchen table drinking a glass of water. I went and got a glass for myself and sat down opposite him.

Tony, I said, what's the story with Tom Bowles? He said you told him things. Like I mentioned Serena's dad and he said you told him what we call him.

Yeah I did. It's not a secret.

Like it's just us, the family and Holly's family. Nobody else calls him that.

Yeah I know. Well Tosser does too and a few of my mates.

So how did you get talking to him?

I just know him, he said. It's none of your business.

But he's a murder suspect, Tony. And you know Dad hates him. If he finds out he'll murder you.

That's all shite. Tom is a nice man. Dad just hates him because of the house, but that's not Tom's fault.

How did you get talking to him?

He looked down at his glass of water. He didn't answer. The lower half of the glass of water was milky-looking. We get that when they put the fluoride in the pipes once a month. There's a smell from it like a swimming pool. It's for our own good. It prevents Dental Caries. I don't know what Dental Caries is or are but I know it's ew so I'm cool with the fluoride. But Holly thinks it is Altering Our Minds and making us Put Up With The Shit The Government Tells Us. It's some kind of mind-control drug. Like I wish they'd control my mind. Holly is totes a conspiracy theorist. She knows who shot John F Kennedy and it wasn't the guy they did for it. The guy that got shot. Lee Harvey Oswald. Shot by Jack Ruby. She says it's just not credible.

Tony?

I told you I met him in a pub? Remember? It wasn't Keniry's. It was Counihan's in town.

Yeah I remember that.

So that's how I got talking to him.

He looked up again and I could see he wasn't going to say any more. So I said, Just I worry about you. Like the time you got in the fight?

That was nothing to do with Tom. I was jumped outside Keniry's.

Who jumped you?

Some langers. I don't know. They were waiting for me. I think they were drinking in Keniry's. They had it in for me. If I get them one by one they'll be sorry.

Where was Tosser?

He was taking a slash in the gents. I was the designated driver.

Tony, can I ask you a question?

He got up and went to the sink. He turned the tap on and let it run cold for a few seconds. Our hot and cold pipes run side by side and the cold pipe always gets hot. Like we have Gold Tap Features and a Fireplace Feature, but anything you can't see is shite. And ever since my dad got mad with the last plumber and went and self-turned up the pressure on the mains there's a knocking when you turn on the cold tap. It's like someone knocking an iron pipe on a stone very fast.

Then he filled the glass of water and drank half of it. He still had his back to me.

The answer is yes, he said. That's why I was jumped.

Cool by me, I said. I just wanted to know. Do Mam and Dad know?

Mam knows. I'm not telling that fucker anything.

That was the first time I realised that Tony properly hated my dad. I couldn't believe I never saw it before. Like when my dad comes into a room Tony leaves. If he can. And Mam is always on his side. And I used to be jealous. But now I understood. Maybe I didn't hate my mam as much as before. But what made them hate each other? I don't know. There was probably a lot going on that I didn't see. The Dog was lying against the Aga watching us with one eye. Tony went over to him and squatted down. How are you, doggy Dog? You don't give a fuck do you as long as you can have a sleep by the heat? He turned around to me. The look on his face was totally sad. I wish I was a dog, he said.

My brother Tony never asked me how I met Tom Bowles and how the nickname of Serena's dad came up. That should have made me think. Like he must already have known how I met him. I could imagine Tom Bowles telling him: I met your sister, she's going to give me an alibi for the murder. I didn't like that idea. But I still didn't know whether Tony went up to Ballyshane. And what did he do up there? I started taking The Dog for a walk again in the evenings after dark, and just like accidentally finding myself in Ballyshane. The lawns were cut now, and someone had been pruning trees. There was a painter's scaffold at one wall and it was half-painted. The place was beginning to look like someone cared. On the first evening I just chilled in the woods for an hour wondering if Tony would turn up, but he didn't so I went home. But the second night I couldn't resist going to the window. It was the kitchen window because that was the only one with lights on. I saw Tom Bowles sitting by a big Aga cooker with a mug of tea in his hands. Grace was cooking. They were watching a small TV high up on the wall. It was the news. Like I think everything they say on the news was written by predictive text. I don't get why people watch it. Like someone is thinking of invading someplace, you just know it will turn out a disappointment. I remember the kitchen because old Miss Corry used to give me tea in there. There was a big pine table with a Formica layer glued on top. There were five pine chairs. The sink was one of those ancient ones that people make flower pots out of. But the cooker was new and it was like one of those huge cookers you see on *MasterChef*. I was impressed. There was a piece of string hung over the stove and there were clothes drying on, shirts and panties and stuff. But what shocked me was there was a bra. A proper bra. Like I didn't expect them to use ordinary bras. That made me look at her again. And this time I was thinking maybe she was a woman after all, just a mannish-looking woman. She had big cheekbones and she was very tall. She looked twice as tall beside Tom Bowles. And she was wearing leggings and a long shirt and when I saw her front I couldn't see any sign of man stuff. I think I concentrated too much because suddenly I noticed that she was looking out the window. The window that had me on the other side of it. Then Tom Bowles turned too. He waved. I panicked. I ran for the woods. The Dog gets excited when I run. He thinks I am Hunting Rabbits or something wild and he barks. He thinks I've finally Come To My Senses and started acting like a proper dog instead of a stupid non-rabbit-aggressive pacifist. So when I got to the trees I tried to shush him but he kept barking and running away from me. I know what it meant in dog psychology: he thought I was giving up too easily on the rabbit confrontation business and he wanted me to go all Semper Fide and Death to Rabbits. But I legged it and he followed me.

So next night that I went up there I stayed away from the window.

It was four nights before Tony turned up. The weather was bad. The met service issued a status yellow warning. Like what did we do before coloured warnings, like when I was young? Weather just happened. Southwest veering-west winds will reach mean speeds sixty-five to eighty km/h with gusts of one hundred and ten km/h., but gusts of up to one hundred and thirty km/h, are likely on exposed coasts and headlands for a time in the evening and early night. Heavy rain later. Ballsyhane is an exposed area. The coast is only a couple of miles away. Like from the top of Ballyshane you can see Lonely Rock Light. When I got up there the trees were heaving and it was roaring like the sea. The wind blew me up the hill, I would probably end up being blown away on my way back.

I was up there jammed against a tree, watching for action. After a bit I started to think I might as well go home. Then my mam's new car came up the drive. I checked my phone and it was still not ten o'clock. Tony got out. He was carrying a large cardboard box. He rang the doorbell and someone let him in. He was there for over an hour and I was actually totally freezing. But eventually I saw him come out again. He was carrying something. He put it in the boot of my mam's car and drove off. I went home. Out through the torrent of the woods, onto the road where the wind almost lifted me off my feet. A few times I had to shelter. Once I held on to a gate. I thought it was going to lift me in the air like Dorothy in *The Wizard of Oz*. I've seen that five times. I love it. It took me nearly an hour to get home. I was soaked. My dad said, Where the hell were you? I said I was walking The Dog and I got lost in the gale. He just gave me the scan.

They were talking about something I could see. I was standing there in the kitchen dripping. My mam was sitting at the kitchen table with a cup of that camomile shit. She thinks it helps her sleep. I hate the smell. My dad was leaning his ass against the sink. He had a glass of something invisible, maybe gin, maybe water. When he joined the Golf Club he started on G&T.

He said, How did Kelleher find out about the Revenue?

My mam said, I'd say everybody knows. These things get around. But I'll tell you one thing, I got a call from the bank yesterday. They wanted to talk to you. They wouldn't talk to me. It's about the farm.

Things get around? Not with the fucking Revenue they don't. There's an informer.

Then the two of them looked at me. One of those looks. If I smoked I would have lit a cigarette as you do. Well, as they do in movies. It has a calming effect. Instead I blushed.

What? I don't even know the Kellehers. They're not in my school.

Did you tell anyone?

Like no? Do you think I want everyone to know we're going bankrupt?

What about the farm, Matt? my mam said. The farm belongs to me.

My dad sort of winked but said nothing.

Did you get a mortgage on the farm, Matt? The Revenue are taking it. If you have a mortgage on that....

How could I get a mortgage on something I don't own?

That's what I was wondering.

I didn't.

My mother fished the bag of soggy camomile out of her cup and dropped it on a saucer. It was steaming. It reminded me of something. I looked up and I saw that Dad was looking at it too.

Shit, he said.

I knew what he was thinking. He gave me a sideways look. I think he was blushing. I could see him standing in the middle of a field pissing and shaking himself dry. We are the complete car-crash family. If something can be screwed up, call us.

The guards called to my house. It was not the same guards who interviewed me. They called after tea and Dad was there too but Mam was working late. They asked my dad if they could talk to me. My dad called me. He said, Suzy, the guards want to talk to you. Ok, Dad. What do they want to talk about? Probably the murder, Dad, remember I found the purse.

I could see my dad was scared. He probably thought they were coming for him when he saw them at the door. The previous day he fired the two people who worked for him. One was a part-timer who came in on Fridays to do the books. That must have been an interesting job. And the other answered the phone and did photocopying, idk, maybe she did something else but she always seemed to be on Facebook when I was there. Or booking her holidays. Maybe there wasn't much to be done in my dad's office anyway. She went on holidays to Italy. She was learning Italian. I want to go to Italy some time. Because the Renaissance of course. And because I love pizza especially not the frozen type.

They interviewed me in the sitting room and my dad waited in the kitchen. They went over my statement about the burning bin. They did not mention that Serena blamed me. They checked each detail. They asked me if I was sure I saw Mr Bowles' housekeeper as well as Mr Bowles. I said I was certain of it. They asked me how come I was so certain? I said the housekeeper is a lot taller than Mr Bowles. They seemed to be cool with that. Then they asked me about the time. I said I was sure about the time because Serena and me waited until everyone was asleep and I told them Serena's theory that people are in their deepest sleep around four a.m. Then they asked me how long it would take to walk up to Ballyshane in the dark. I estimated half an hour, and fifteen minutes by day. They said they had checked with the alarm people and there was no record of an alarm because the system was not monitored. I said I didn't know that, but it made a lot of noise. It was one of those old-fashioned alarms with a bell on it. They asked me if I knew that the alarm in Ballyshane had been recently replaced and the house was now fitted with motion sensors and cameras. I said I didn't know that, but the night we set fire to the bin it was still the old alarm. Then they asked me about my dad freaking when I came home. And I said it was true. And they said they would need my dad to confirm that. And I started to cry.

And my dad said he had no recollection of it. I couldn't believe he said that. Like, Dad you totally freaked at me, when I got home, like I thought you were going to have another heart attack. My dad said it was his opinion that what I was saying was not the truth.

I looked at him and I saw that half smile again.

The cop said, Mr Regan, are you aware that your daughter provided two suspects with an alibi for the night in question and if you can't confirm her story then the alibi is dead in the water?

My father nodded. You're talking about Bowles, he said. I always thought that guy was suspicious.

Dad, I said, what are you doing?

He ignored me. Can I offer you tea or coffee, Sergeant? Or a drop of something stronger, sure I know you're on duty, but still and all?

They said no thanks. They just needed to clarify here. Was he saying that he did not remember his daughter coming home in the early hours of the morning on the night in question, or was he saying it didn't happen?

My dad thought hard. You knew when he was thinking hard because he frowned. Then he looked at me and looked away again.

Could I speak to you alone, he said to the guards.

For fuck's sake, Dad!

Suzy! Language! Just go and wait in the kitchen will you. There's a good girl.

If you wouldn't mind, miss, the older of the two guards said.

I went into the kitchen. But then I came back and listened at the door. The older guard's voice was louder than the others. I heard him say, So now just to be clear, you're saying they're a bit high strung?

And then my dad said something and the older guard said, Is that a fact? That's very sad. And her father a surgeon too. You never know what's behind it.

Then I heard them moving. I went back to the kitchen. I heard them saying thanks and sorry for disturbing him and goodbye now thanks very much.

The younger guard stuck his head in at the kitchen door and said, Thanks very much there, Suzy. You were very helpful.

I waited until they were gone. Then I went up to my room and closed the door quietly. I went to look for my blades but I heard Dad coming up after me so instead I threw myself on the bed looking away. I heard the door open.

Are you all right, Suzy?

I know what you did.

Suzy you know very well I was only just after my operation and I was taking sleeping tablets. I don't remember anything.

That's not what you told the guards though. You could have told them that while I was there. I heard what you said. And I know what you're doing.

I just don't remember.

I turned around and looked straight at him. Mam is right about you.

That hit him. He backed out and closed the door hard. I jumped up and pulled my chair over and propped it against the handle. He waited for a few seconds and he tried the handle of the door but I pushed hard against the chair. Then I heard him go downstairs and not long afterwards I heard him on the phone. I took a blade and dropped my pants and very quickly made two short slashes across the front of my thighs. I watched the blood well up in the slits and run down onto the cover of my duvet. A bright pink stain spread and got deeper in colour. I wanted to do it again but the pain was already too much. I threw the blade on the floor and rolled over onto my side. I realised I was crying. I was bleeding all over the bed.

I dreamed a horse was kicking down a door and I woke up and it was someone trying to break into my room. It was dark. I was scared. I called out, Who's there? and my brother Tony answered. When I rolled over I realised one of my legs was stuck to the duvet. I had my pants down around my knees. I was cold. I remembered what I was doing before I fell asleep. I told Tony to hang on. I gently pulled the duvet off my cut and pulled my pants up. Maybe I bled again idk. When I moved my legs it hurt. I turned the duvet upside down to hide the blood and pulled the chair out from under the door handle. Tony came in.

What are you doing in the dark?

I turned my bedside light on. I saw him looking at my legs. There was blood on my skinnies. Then he looked at the blade on the floor.

Oh Jesus no, he said. Why did you do that? He was pointing at my legs.

My fucking life, I said. Dad just told the guards I was a liar.

About what?

You know about the bin, right?

He stared at me. He told them you were lying about that?

He said I was highly strung. He said he didn't remember me coming home late that night. He told them that Serena overdosed.

He turned and ran down the stairs. I heard him in the lounge, then in the kitchen. Things were getting knocked over. Chairs maybe idk. Doors slammed. The kitchen door. Then he started shouting, Dad! Dad! Where the fuck are you? Where the fuck are you, you lying cunt!

I don't know where my dad was, but Tony went through every room. There was no one else there except him and me and The Dog.

So I dated Jack. It was a bad idea and I don't know why I did it. Don't even ask. I even shaved my legs for the first time. I used my Dad's Mach 3 razor even though my mam has a Gillette Venus Spa Breeze, lathers for lush smoothness + indulgent shave gel bars. Like is that even a thing? A shave gel bar? And why do we have to use pink ones? Do pink razors have gentler blades? I used my mam's shampoo. Sunkist Raspberry. Who puts raspberries in their hair? Is that even a thing? It smelled like raspberry ice-cream not in a good way. Like the cheapest raspberry ice-cream. I was worried that he might want to smell my hair. Or even nibble my ear. It happens. But I needn't have worried. He didn't give a shit about my hair.

As soon as he found a place to park he got me into the the back seat of his mother's car and it wasn't very nice. He was all hands and some of it hurt idk he tried to get his hand under my bra and my skinnies were too tight and I wasn't going to open the button ffs. In the end I just told him piss off. I don't think a girl ever did that before. He was surprised. He made me swear not to tell Serena. As far as I was concerned she was welcome to him. I already worked out he was an asshole from the second I got in the car. The funny thing is, while he was kissing me, and trying to get me to touch his thingy, and accidentally on purpose getting his hand stuck in my skinnies, I was thinking of a chapter in my Physics book about X-rays. Like high-energy particles, hot cathode ray tubes, electromagnetic waves, ionisation, penetration. I almost laughed out loud a few times. No way are you supposed to be thinking about Physics. It was all a bit awkward frankly. But the best part of it was when he knocked over the can of beer that was jammed in the cup holder. It went on the driver's seat. He said his mother would kill him. He spent ten minutes trying to clean it off. And when he showed me how he had made shit of the seat by spreading the stain I shook my head and said, Tsk tsk that's terrible. He had to sit in the wet to drive me home. I thought that was hilarious but he didn't. And then he left me home and it was only nine o'clock in the night. Like the whole thing happened in two hours, including the valeting. I guess he's just a sensitive guy. I wonder if he sleeps with the light on? In twenty years time he'd be voting for idk Opus Dei Lite or the Illuminati whatever, if you've seen the *Da Vinci Code* you get the idea, and passing around pics of aborted foetuses like business cards. Like all of our political parties are Opus Dei Lite. It's hard to get away from it here.

When I got home I texted Holly to say I was out with Jack. I know I said I never would but I'm crap at secrets. And Holly is my soul.

And she texted me back: Well?

And I replied: Nope just groped.

I WhatsApped her a selfie of me and Jack just to prove it. He was making a funny face that was not funny. He looked like a wanker pretending to be a wanker. A selfie never lies. And she was like: Wat was it like? And I said: It was ew n he's a shit. She said: ☹. I said it was OK because I preferred her and she replied: Hehehe ☺. So then she wanted to know the gory details, about where he put his hand and some other more personal things. I said it was all a bit meh. I told her how fast he was and she quoted me back the same song. He's just a sensitive guy. I answered the other questions too. Then I told her that he wanted to go home as soon as he realised I wouldn't do it and she said: I knew hed be like that. total fucking buffer.

And I did too. But I replied, Harsh hehe.

The last thing Holly texted before we said our goodnights was: Sleepover tomorrow night? Tell me all about it? And I said: Awesome girl. Then it was goodnight and sleep tight and the rest of it. But the one thing I didn't tell Holly was that Jack asked me if my brother could sell him hash. I said he'd have to ask him himself. He said, They say the Ballyshane guy has the best of it, that's where Tony gets it. It was news to me. All of it.

That night Tony knocked on my door very late. I was already asleep and by the way he was knocking I guessed my parents were asleep too. He came in and I made room for him in the bed. The last time Tony was in my bed we were like babies, I was six and he was ten maybe. I could smell drink on his breath but I don't think he was drunk. He made himself comfortable, with his back against the wall. He was fully dressed. I could smell cigarette smoke from his clothes. I legit hate cigarette smoke, especially the used version. But he's my brother.

He didn't say anything for a bit. I knew he was working up to something. Like the last heart-to-heart I had with Tony I was probably two and a half. It was funny really.

What it was, he wanted my advice. Like MY advice? Me the walking catastrophe, with the emphasis on the ASS. He should or he should not tell Dad?

I gave it some thought. After a bit he's like: Suzy are you asleep?

I said, I'm thinking.

Well you fucking sound like you're asleep.

Harsh. How could I be talking to you if I was asleep?

You could be talking in your sleep.

I hit him but it didn't hurt. He said OW anyway just to please me. Aw. Big brothers.

I said, I think you should tell him. He might be mad but he'll get over it.

OK, he said. I suppose.

Well, what's the worst case scenario? He tells you move out? He never wants to talk to you again? Like if you move out, take me with you.

I bitch-slapped him on the shoulder and said, J and K must be determined from the output states of the J-K flip-flop.

I could see he didn't get it. It's from your textbook!

Suzy, seriously, you worry me sometimes. What fucking textbook?

We had a laugh about that. I asked him about being gay. What was it like? Did he have gay friends? How would one gay person know another gay person if he saw him? How many gay people would I know? Like among my circle of acquaintances. Did he ever make a pass at straight guys? Are gay men attracted to lesbian women? Like, what is it about women that gay men don't like?

I asked him if he ever went to gay clubs.

Sometimes, he said. Not a lot though. There's only one anyway.

I told him I saw all that on telly. Gay clubs and dancing and all that. But I was wondering if they dress up for it. Some guys in dresses and high heels and some girls in suits? And trannies. All that shit. Talking funny.

And would you see guys kissing guys? And is it all mad active and up? Like to judge by the telly gays have all the fun. I was trying to remember where I saw that. I think it was a documentary about an American guy.

Not really, he said. It's a pretty quiet place. Like a pub, you know? There's a bit of a dance floor.

Me: So that's where you met the Bowles guy?

Tony: No that was in Counihans's. Remember? I told you. He came in with his daughter.

Me: His daughter?

Tony: Yeah, Grace.

Me: Grace is a woman? Are you sure?

Tony: Listen, just because I'm gay…

Me: But she's twice his size?

Tony: What has that got to do with anything?

Me: So you liked him because he's gay?

Tony: He's not gay.

Me: Are you sure?

Tony: Bowles had three wives.

Me: Really? Wow.

Tony: The second time I met him was after you and Serena broke in…

Me: We didn't break in we only broke a window!

Tony: And burned his bin to the ground.

Me: OK, we burned his bin too. Serena is a pyromaniac.

Well, he needed his alarm fixed and I told him I was in Elec Eng and one thing followed another and I ended up installing the new alarm system for him. That's how I got to know him.

You installed his alarm system?

It's easy peasy. It's like a kit. You could do it yourself.

Tony, have you got a boyfriend?

He giggled. I never heard Tony giggle before. I wondered if it was a gay thing and he just like kept it to himself until he talked to me. Like maybe he always giggled inside but being in the closet it wasn't something he could do in public. And then I wondered if I was in a closet too. Maybe I was lesbian. The Jack Thing was certainly not fab. Maybe you couldn't really get to know a boy the way Holly and me knew each other. Like boys are about football and computer games. About Which I Knew Fuck All. And they were always whacking each other and bitching at each other. But now that I thought of it I only ever heard Tony laughing when he was with Tosser and the guys. And then it had to be that male shit laughing. Because peer pressure.

It's not Tosser is it? I couldn't stand having him in the family. I mean Tosser is OK, but you know what I mean. Well-named like.

But it wasn't Tosser.

It's not Great-To-Meet Micky's eldest is it? I saw you with him the other day.

That fucking langer? Give me some credit, Suzy!

It turned out to be someone I didn't know. And it wasn't def yet. He'd let me know if it came right. And I asked him when he planned to tell Dad and he said he needed to pick the right time. And I said there would never be a right time. Like Tony is supposed to be a scion of the realm. My dad still thinks he's doing real

Engineering and will grow up to be someone who builds stuff. But in Elec, a fact that seems to have escaped my dad's attention, they don't build houses. They don't even do the wiring.

Then he told me he heard something. It might have been a joke. Don't ever tell Dad, he said, but he wanted to know how come Kelleher sold so fast.

It's his *casus belli*, I said. We did *casus belli* when we did Bismarck.

What the fuck is *casus belli*?

Nevermind, just tell me.

Bowles let it slip that he dropped Kelleher a serious wad of cash. Under the table.

Fuck.

He said he understood that was how business was done in Ireland.

It legit is too. All the politicians are on the take. Remember whatsisname with the Charvet shirts? And all that gang? They're only the ones that got caught. Dad does it too.

Does he?

I went silent. I didn't know for sure.

Bowles is dangerous, he said. Don't mess with him again.

Why is he dangerous? He's practically a midget. He's like totally challenged.

Just leave him alone.

And after that he told me what happened with John Brown. I said I didn't want to know. It was too sad. I don't ever think of John Brown if I can help it because it

261

makes me cry. The last time I deliberately thought about him was his anniversary and I cried all day. And reading the book he gave me didn't help. But he said he wanted me to know. He had to tell someone.

Don't tell me. Tell Tosser.

Tosser knows.

Well, don't tell anyone for fuck's sake. Keep it secret. Like you're out of the closet now, put the story of John Brown into the closet instead and close the door.

Suzy listen. It was an accident.

I could feel him shaking in the bed beside me. He couldn't have been cold, he was fully dressed. Then I realised he was crying. He had one hand in a fist against his face. I put an arm around him idk I never cuddled my brother, he's my big brother ffs, but I put my arm around him and gave him like a serious hug. We're not a hugging family. If my mam gave me a hug I would like die. It would be so embarrassing. Like there is this thing in science called hydrophobicity, which is that certain molecules have the property of repelling water. Well, when they put our family together they made one of our properties hug-o-phobicity. And maybe not telling people anything. And fighting.

What's not generally known is that there is no force in hydrophobicity molecules. They don't repel water. It's just there is nothing to draw them together. If they were humans they would just be cold. I googled it. Once upon a time.

I heard him peeing and brushing his teeth. Like a horse peeing into a bucket. Why don't boys sit down? And then I heard him get into bed. I am the observing angel. Nothing happens in my house that I don't know about. And no one can sleep until I hear them close their eyes. Sometimes I think I hold the house in my hand and maybe the whole world. If I open my fingers it falls through the cracks. If I close my fist everyone dies.

Best year worst year favourite food.

I fell asleep eventually and I dreamed about John Brown. Surprise surprise. Like these days I have mice in my dreams. And floating beams. I dream the weirdest things. But if I could order a good dream from Amazon it would contain John Brown.

So they arrested some guy who worked in the accounts department of Lidl. Choose to live a little, as the ad says. Maybe he shouldn't have swallowed his own crappy advertising. It was on the news. The guards must have believed my story and not Dad's. That was a surprise. I didn't think anyone believed me ever. And even I don't believe Serena. And everyone in my school was like, OMG he was packing shelves when I was there, I saw him. Or, OMG he was looking right at me. This is my school, which is one hundred per cent girl except for a few teachers like Leary who doesn't count. We All Saw Him And He Looked Straight At Us. Several girls knew he was an axe-murderer or whatever all along. They felt it, like The Force or something, like they just sensed that he was a rapist. As you do. There was a even a few thought he was nice. And someone in second year was Related To Him By Marriage. Her third cousin was married to the guy's aunt.

And Serena called me up one day and asked if we could be friends again and she was sorry and she loved me and she would never want to hurt me. Ever.

First I said, Whatevs, and then I got conscience and said I was sorry too.

I didn't know what we were sorry about, but it doesn't hurt to apologise for something you can't remember. So she started crying on the phone. She has a liquidity problem big time. She's a full-time crisis. She said she felt so guilty but she wouldn't say why. I guessed it was because of all the lies. So I said, So you're not pregnant? And that only made it worse. It was legit impossible to understand a word she said. Except towards the end she said, I did something awful, I'm so sorry. Then she hung up.

And by then Holly was actually dating Tosser, which was so totally random I couldn't believe it. Like dating Tosser is crossing the very last red line of all the red lines. Is it even possible for a human? Who knew it could happen? I asked her if they'd done it and she just smiled. Like nobody tells me anything. It was May and the exams were coming close and everybody was a bit stressed. I went to Serena's house and we were going to study together. Like Serena is almost as good as me except she doesn't have the photographic memory shit. She really has to work hard at it. Her dad wasn't there and her mam was out at some Morning, like a Coffee Morning or a Gin Morning, whatever kind of Mornings she does. She was in a Book Club too, as well as the Golf Club and the Tennis Club and the Sailing Club. The Mornings were usually For Charity. She was in the Lions Club. She's the kind of mother you read about on Mumsnet.

Serena couldn't believe Holly and Tosser were going out. Like Tosser is twenty-two and Holly is eighteen. I said there was no law against it. She asked me if they did anything and I said I didn't ask Holly about that, it was her business. Like, were they even kissing? She couldn't imagine Holly being a good kisser. I said, Oh she's a good kisser all right, the best.

Oh fuck, Serena said, you did her didn't you? You did her and you wouldn't do me. Bitch I own you.

I shrugged. I said nothing. She stared at me. Then she said, I want one lesbian experience before I marry Jack.

This was news to me.

Why would you marry Jack?

He's the father of my baby.

I looked at her. She was like totally flat. She didn't even have a tummy. I said, You're not pregnant.

I am.

You don't look it.

It's not showing yet. I missed my last two periods.

I looked at her again. Even for three months she was too flat. Maybe she was a bit bigger on top. My cousin was completely flat until about three months though, and later she was huge. She had preeclampsia. I googled it. It is serious. On Mumsnet it is like nuclear. Everybody was worried but it all went fine in the end and the baby is a dote. Her name is Eve. Holly says they should have called her Adam and the next one Eve. First things first, she says.

I decided that Serena needed me to believe she was pregnant. It's probably a Condition. Mumsnet has the deal on phantom pregnancies. It is called pseudocyesis. I think Serena has pseudocyesis and a lot of other pseudos.

266

We all have Conditions idk maybe psychologists could diagnose us. I decided she needed me to imagine a baby inside her so she could imagine it herself. Like I'm independent confirmation that her nightmare-fantasy is an actual baby and not a phantom.

Did you tell your dad?

She shook her head. I'm scared.

I said, At least you won't have to tell him until after the exams. You look totally non-pregnant. In a month you'll be done with your last paper and you can tell him then. You'll have a bump by then.

I asked her if she could feel anything and she said it was too early. She googled it and you generally don't start to feel movement until between sixteen and twenty-two weeks. Eventually she'll have to pay attention to the movements because if he doesn't move for a while he might be in distress. She looked dreamy talking about it. Like mothers with babies in them look totally stoned sometimes. I was jealous. I made her promise that as soon as she felt something she was to tell me so I could feel it too.

I texted Holly: Serena says she's preg Jack is the dad.

Holly: She's always worse on her period and she's on now.

Me: Rolls eyes.

The other topic of conversation was my brother's boyfriend who by now everybody knew about except my dad. His name is Páraic. He was a teacher from the boys' school, a man of thirty years of age, and very good-looking. I just don't get how all the best-looking guys are gay. Except John Brown. It was going on a couple of weeks now and they were not hiding anything. The word was that the principal of the boys' school was gutted and was looking at ways of getting rid of Páraic but it was illegal. The principal's nickname was Snotty. Boys do that. He had a habit of rubbing his nose when he was talking. Serena said she didn't think you could be a native Irish speaker and gay at the same time. We thought that was so funny. Like to listen to our Irish teacher, every Irish speaker was a Catholic and Very Good and Said The Rosary After Tea All The Mysteries and Never Even Tasted Alcohol. I said Páraic was striking a blow for freedom. But that wasn't funny because it was actually true.

Páraic picked Tony up from college and dropped him home most days. Which meant Tony actually had to go to lectures. Tony was even talking about moving in with him. He has a flat not owned by my dad. It was a nice place with a sea view. Not Executive Home standard nice, but nice all the same. Him and Tony brought me to dinner there one day. He has a big window and you can see ships going up the channel to the city docks. Páraic is a good cook. We had crab soup to start. Like I don't know about crab, it's seriously unlike anything you should eat. And the eyes are something else. You could get them in *Aliens* where they would emerge from Sigourney Weaver's bellybutton. But the soup was OK and basically you couldn't tell it was crab because there was no shell. Then some kind of vegetable thing for mains and strawberry pavlova for dessert. The pavlova was fab. Pavlova is my all-time fave.

So I like him. He is a Science teacher. He is qualified to teach Science through Irish which must be really weird. I mean I know there has to be a word for everything, but like how would you say Large Hadron Collider for example? Or what's the Irish for the output states of J-K flip-flops?

Serena asked me about Tony. It was the same question I asked her. When is he going to tell my dad? I said I didn't know. He was waiting until my dad got the all clear about the stent. Technically his heart is still in recovery. Anyway, my mam was cool with it and my dad is not the noticing type. Not unless Tony's boyfriend had a For Sale sign attached and maybe on-street parking.

So I totally didn't believe in being pregnant and having a period at the same time, which Serena was like, I didn't have my period for two months. And I was like, Holly said you were on. And Serena flipped.

And I was also not believing in the three times a night anymore. The way I saw it, if Jack did her once that was him sorted and his next thought would be, Hello, hello, we are the Chelsea boys. Sex first then Chelsea FC. And Serena was way too cool. If I was pregnant, and I wasn't because (a) my two periods were dead on time and (b) I didn't let Jack do it, which is a killer where pregnancy is concerned, I would be jumping. But if pretending to be pregnant was good for her, it was OK by me too.

As a matter of fact Jack keeps texting me. Suzy story? wanna do sthing on firday night? I never reply. He is a wanker.

We did some work. After about an hour she said, Can I ask you something?

I said there was no harm in asking.

When you showed me your cuts, like, are you still cutting?

I said no. I was clean for two months at that point.

In fact I stopped after the night I slashed myself. The night Dad lied to the guards in the hope of getting Tom Bowles arrested and getting a chance to buy Ballyshane again. That was soooo weird, my dad getting this big plot going in which he was going to frame an innocent man for a murder he did not commit. It could have been *The Fugitive* but really it was like something out of *Only Fools and Horses* which is on repeat again and which I love. I totally want to marry Rodney Trotter. I can't resist a plonker.

What about you?

Naw, she said, I'm clean too.

But I knew she wasn't. I said, Did Jack see your scars?

She said he did. He was cool with them. He said it made him love her more. He had cuts on his thighs too but he said that he hadn't done anything since they started going out.

I didn't say anything. I didn't even think of rolling my eyes.

Serena was making mental teddy bears. We all make mental teddy bears for comfort. Otherwise everything would be unbearable. We are girls and we are surrounded by people who want to do things to us. That is the world. Just think about it. Imagine you're a seventeen-year-old boy in football shorts walking down a dark road at night. It's a country road. Cars are passing on their way home from the pub. Now imagine you're a girl in a miniskirt.

Who made this world the way it is? Not Serena or me or Holly. We're just trying to get along, making things up as we go, little stories to make the night seem friendly.

What will your dad say?

She thought for a minute. She was looking at a page of French verbs, *présent, futur, futur antérieur, imparfait, passé composé, passé simple, conditionnel*. She's crap at French. Then she said, I don't know what the future holds but just now I need to be strong.

I thought, What crap! I knew she would say something like that. I almost expected her to point at the future tense. *Je serai, tu seras, il sera*. Deep down Serena is shallow. She is the Princess of Cliché.

I looked at her. She had straw-coloured hair that was thin and totally straight. She never even had to use a straightener. Her eyes were a sort of hazel brown. She had thin straight lips. Like her figure was perfect because she never ate anything. Once she was sort of curvy, sort of chubby, and then about twelve she downsized big time. She went from curvy to svelte and recently it was skin and bones. The skin and bones happened without me noticing. I am not the best noticer. She would make a great model, like she already has the anorexia and the drug habit. All she does is pick at food, but she can pick at it in such a way that people think she's eating. She was still staring at the verbs.

Then she said, I'm crap at the conditional.

Me too, I said, me too.

Like what's the difference between *je serai* and *je serais*? How would you know which is which? I don't even know how to pronounce them.

Beats me, I said.

She started to cry. I put my arm around her. She just cried there for a bit. And then she said she was sorry and I said it was OK. I took my own tissue from my sleeve and dried her eyes. For two seconds I thought she was going to kiss me which would be idk maybe ew, but then maybe not, but then she didn't. And we started on our books again. And ten minutes later her dad came home. I heard the front door opening and quiet footsteps. Serena stopped breathing until she heard a door close somewhere else. Probably his office.

I'm on a new tablet, she said. I'm much better now.

All the stories we couldn't tell our fathers. Like practically my whole life. The day he found out about Tony was the worst day ever. Like the absolute worst, even worse than what happened after. I don't know how it started. These things get leaked. Someone said something at the club or some fucking club. Like, I see your lad is a homo, Mattie boy. Something friendly in a gin-and-tonic press-the-flesh press release in the Green Room of Castlemartin fucking Golf Club. Freedom of information. I know what they say about gay people. It is seriously hard to be around people sometimes.

I wasn't there when he found out and I wasn't there when he got home. When he exploded.

Like maybe he expected grandchildren or something. Someone he could love in his old age when love finally caught up with him. Or maybe he expected a strategic marriage so he could own the only daughter of an Audi dealership as well as a million houses. Just lately, I think I hated him more than my mother. Only I never knew.

Then everything happened so fast. Once upon a time I was watching a hawk or a kestrel idk and he was just doing nothing, like he was a baby's mobile, just hanging in the sky, and then I blinked and he was falling. I know he killed something because I heard it. It was like a micro-scream.

I was out walking with Holly. I was giving her a grind in the Weimar Republic. I called it my pedestrian grind, because we were getting some fresh air at the same time. I have Weimar nailed. And my phone rang. It was Tony.

Suzy, can you come home? Like now?

I could hear something in his voice. Maybe panic.

What's the story?

Dad found out.

Oh shit.

Yeah. Like he went ballistic. Suzy I'm scared.

I had my bike. It was ten minutes from Holly's house. I made it in six. As soon as I came through the door I could hear my dad shouting up the stairs. A queer! A fucking queer in my family! With a man, a teacher! The whole town knows. Come down here you dirty shite and I'll straighten you out. Jesus fucking Christ.

And I could hear my mam crying.

Then my dad heard me behind him. He turned around and pointed at me. You knew? You knew didn't you?

I just nodded my head. I was too scared to talk.

Jesus Christ the whole fucking family knew! A bumboy? Do you know he goes up to that bastard at night? Do you know where he buys his fucking drugs?

What bastard, Dad?

Fucking Bowles. He goes up to Ballyshane. I don't even want to know what he does to him. LIKE WHAT SERVICES DOES HE PROVIDE TO THAT CUNT?

My mam came out. She was hiding in the bathroom but when she heard me she got courage. Matt, calm down or you'll damage your valves. Calm down!

Fuck my valves! I want that sack of shit down here. I want him to tell me to my face what he is. Then I'm going to throw the bastard out. He'll never darken my door again.

I'm calling the doctor, my mam said.

I heard it in the Golf Club for Jesus sake. In the fucking club.

I don't know why she was calling the doctor but whatever she did it couldn't be worse than listening to this crap. My dad looked at her. Call the fucker, he said, I don't give a shit.

Then I heard Tony calling me. Suzy, are you down there?

Then his door opened. Suzy?

My father started up the stairs at a run but he only got to the fifth step. Then he stopped. He sat down suddenly. My mam screamed.

She handed me the phone. Call an ambulance!

I didn't know what to do.

Nine nine nine, she said. Do it!

But my dad said no, he was fine, he didn't even have a pain. His voice sounded like there was too much air in. Suddenly I could hear that the whole universe had switched to silent running. Nothing was making any kind of sound, not even the smallest bird. My dad looked a bit bleached out. He came down again. Step by step. He was very quiet and his voice was a bit low. He went into the lounge and sat down and Mam and me went in after him. My mam pulled a stool up and lifted his feet onto it. He looked a bit shocked. He kept saying he was all right. My mam said she would get him a glass of water, but when she was in the kitchen I heard her talking to the doctor on her mobile. Tony came down. He looked terrified. He peeped into the lounge but he didn't go in. I whispered to him that he should get his things and just go to his boyfriend's and when things settled down I'd call him. So that's what he did and my mam let him take her car. And then the doctor came and he examined my dad and he called an ambulance and they took him in and my mam and me followed them in the Lexus, only slower because we didn't have flashing lights and a siren. And when we got to the hospital they were already prepping him for the operating theatre. And my mam held one of his hands and I held the other. And all that time he didn't say anything. And his eyes just moved around very fast but not as if he was looking at things. More like a bird idk. I was scared tbh. And my mam said she loved him and then I did too, although I can't be sure that I meant it, and all I wanted him to do was say it back, and say he loved Tony too. But he never said anything.

The only house my dad didn't let was Clarinda Park. After the funeral we had to clear it out and there was a locked cupboard. I was scared. My mam got a hammer and chisel and chiselled out the lock. She was good at it. Who would have guessed. It was a Saturday and the air was grey with water, not rain, just some sort of wet airy stuff that made it hard to breathe. The cupboard was full of clothes. I recognised the ratty old cardigan he used to wear before Mam bought him a V-neck cashmere sweater, which he then wore like forever. It looked like everything old ended up here. Even a pair of golf shoes. Mam looked at me. I think the look said: What am I going to do now? Or maybe it was: Did we ask for this? Idk I can't read other people. I'm so wrong so often. It's hard enough to know what to do with dead people's clothes, but what are you supposed to do with dead people's dead clothes that they kept from a previous life? I could smell my dad. It was an all closed-up smell, Dad's old clothes mixed with IKEA-wardrobe-smell and stale-golf-club-grass and sadness. It was old people sad. It was the worst kind.

I cried.

My mam got some plastic bin bags and we started to put the things into it. At the very back behind everything there was an envelope with an iPhone in it. It was powered down. We turned it on but it was password protected and it wasn't Dad's usual. Then at the very bottom, stuffed into a sock, was a pair of panties. My mam asked me if it was mine. It was too small for her, she said. Like how would I know? I have a million panties. And basically panties are panties. There's only like ten different kinds. But why would my dad have a pair of my panties in an old sock?

My mam told me to go downstairs and put the kettle on. I knew what she was doing. She was worried. She wanted to empty the rest of the place on her own. So I made the tea and brought her up a mug and she was sitting on the bed trying passwords on the iPhone and crying. I sat down beside her and hugged her.

Mam, I said, he always had two phones.

I know, she said, but they're both at home in his desk.

I kept the panties. I googled them. *Byzance thong lingerie range by Simone Pérèle brand.* The advertising is barely literate. *Byzance thong an elegant and innovative for every demanding women. A Byzance line especially conceived for their easiness to wear their comfort and excellent support.* Thirty-nine euro. Like my expensive panties are Marks & Sparks three-in-a-pack sort of fake silk idk whatever they make fake silk out of. But these have lace in the front, a lot of lace, like lace almost all the way down ^_^. Their easiness to wear. And maybe easiness to take off.

I wondered if Miss Morocco wore thongs.

I tried them on which was ew frankly but they were size small and I'm medium. So they definitely were not mine.

The Lingerie Rooms are the ultimate destinations for all your lingerie, hosiery, shapewear and swimwear needs. Choose from over seventy brands with many exclusives. We have expert lingerie fitters across all stores who will ensure the best fit, ultimate comfort and tailored solutions, so you feel fabulous whatever the occasion.

I wondered about a career as lingerie fitter in one of the lingerie rooms. I looked at some of the models and wouldn't mind helping them fit their panties and bras. Helping her to feel fabulous no matter what the occasion. I got quite into googling lingerie. I missed Dad. I could have sneaked one of his cards and bought a few on Amazon.

I didn't tell Mam. She was still trying to work out how a pair of my knickers got into Dad's sock and her best theory is that it happened in the wash.

Peter came to the funeral. I texted him to say my dad died and he came all the way up. He stood beside me when they were putting my dad into the hole.

Tom Bowles and his daughter came to the funeral. They were like the couple in the Bible. David and Goliath. Except if Goliath was a woman. Maybe Goliath was a woman idk I'm reserving judgement after the arse up I made about Grace. After the burial, when people started the sympathy business, all forming a single line and approaching the bereaved, namely us, Tom Bowles shook hands with my mam. I could see he didn't know what to do. Like definitely all the priest stuff was news to him. I said to Serena, Ghost writers probably don't do funerals. But she didn't see the joke. He shook my hand too and he winked at me. Can you even do that at a funeral? And then his daughter shook my hand and idk I thought she held on to it a bit long. But it was OK. Maybe. Anyway she was way too tall for me. Then she shook hands with Serena and Serena said she wasn't related to the deceased and the daughter just blushed.

Holly came to the funeral. Only for Holly. She is the best. She held my hand like it was made of glass. She would never break it.

Even Miss Morocco came. I saw her at the back of the crowd, a little piece of grace and calm way out by the railings. She had her baby in a sling. I wanted to talk to her. I wanted to ask her about my dad. Like did he have a good side? But families of dead people have a duty to stand at the edge of the grave until the whole shaking hands thing is over. By then she was gone.

My mam never cried the funeral.

I made up for her though. Holly gave me tissues. And Serena was totalled. I whispered: Get a grip, Serena, FFS he was MY dad not yours.

And she sobbed out loud: I'm sorry, I'm sorry.

FFS.

People were probably thinking: Did someone die on her too?

I always cry. I cried John Brown's like shit and I cried my grandad's.

Serena is as white as the snow. I don't know why I love her but I do. I thought she was the one who would die first. She is so thin I don't know what's holding her up, even if she has bones any more, and her eyes have that greyed-out look like ashes. Tbh she looks like a biter from the *Walking Dead*. She cried when she saw me crying and we hugged and hugged. She still does not look pregnant and idk which is better to be pregnant and her dad will kill her or to think being pregnant is better than being Serena all alone. Then my mam announced that there would be refreshments at the hotel and Serena whispered to me, I'm getting morning sickness bad. And over her shoulder I saw Dan Kelleher the auctioneer in his Crombie overcoat, standing at the very back. And I started to wonder, who would the Revenue employ to sell my dad's houses? And I wondered if he'd get Castlemartin now. Now that my dad wasn't pissing on him any more.

And there was like a funeral party in the hotel. On the way there in the back seat of idk a funeral car, like a funeral car is also a wedding car, my mam put her arm around me and said we all needed to stick together, we'd manage. I didn't want to kill her any more. Enough death already my conscience said to me. She still had her job, she said, and Computing Solutions was being very good. She had funeral leave or something. We would manage. Maybe she always loved me, who knows. I never know anything in my family. And tbf I don't think she hates me. Not really. It's just I'm some kind of a disappointment to her.

I've been to three funeral parties now and they are all the same except John Brown's was a trillion times sadder. The hotel puts up a table with sandwiches, usually ham and maybe smoked salmon. I assume the bereaved family is shelling out for that – we the bankrupts in this case. Everybody buys drink which is where the hotel scores. And first people are sad and they talk quietly, but after the second drink happiness breaks out. In one hour everyone is chatting about their holidays or their grandkids or the ponies or the match. People tell jokes. If it runs late someone will sing 'The Rising Of The Moon' or 'The Boys Who Beat The Black And Tans'. Everybody feels good about beating The Black And Tans. Like they are everybody's love-to-hate historical persons, next to Hitler. At least where I live. But we don't have any songs about Hitler in Ireland.

But all the people who actually did those things and fought those fights are dead. My grandad knew them. Now all that's left is the Gobshite Party, never mind what colour. My grandad used to say the old fighters would have put the present government against a wall and plugged them. My grandad used to say plugged. Aw I miss him.

Peter was the most popular person in the room. Everybody said wasn't he great to come so far. He was offering to deliver turf and people were interested. Or they were pretending to be interested idk.

I went to the toilet and rang my brother. I told him I missed him and he should be here. He said: Listen, Suzy, Dad was a shit, I was never good enough for him, he totally hated me, I think he knew I was gay before I did myself. Maybe even when I was a kid. And he fucking despised me, right? Don't lie about it, Suzy. He just hated me. I'm trying to get myself together and if I never remember him again it's all the same to me. You were always his favourite, it's easy for you, girl.

That just made me cry again. I just kept saying, I miss you, I miss you.

Eventually someone came in and went into the next cubicle and I had to hang up. And whoever it was, they didn't come in there to pee either. And when I came out it was evening. There was a bloody sunset, clouds streaked across it. I thought of all the things we had done to our bodies, Serena and Tony and me. My dad too. Holly is the pure one. The world is possible because she exists. I have the darkness on me.

Mam asked Tony to hack the Clarinda Park phone but he said the FBI couldn't hack an iPhone so how could he. He took it away with him. He brought it back three days later and told us he couldn't do it. He told us that Páraic suggested we take turns guessing the password. It was the only way. Like we needed a secondary school teacher to tell us that. Mam said she already spent hours trying to guess it. Tony said the same. Then they looked at me.

Like I didn't know his old passcode.

My mam walked across the kitchen and put the phone into my hand. I pressed the home button. Enter Passcode. I put my birthday in. I tried it several ways. It didn't work.

I took it up to my bedroom and started putting in random passcodes. I texted Holly about it. She said the combinations were probably in millions. Like where does Holly get this information? She said I should try my Dad's numbers – birthdays, bank numbers, car numbers, telephone numbers. So I started trying any that I knew. Later she texted me that her dad said I should try my friend's birthdays.

Me: WTF??? My dad doesn't even remember my friend's names.

After I sent I remembered I should have said didn't. I cried of course. I cry ffs what's new. I missed my dad. Like idk why, he was having a fucking affair, he was hiding some woman's knickers in his sock, he bankrupted the family idk I shouldn't fucking care. Sometimes I think I hear him in his office. On the phone he was always half-shouting. He didn't get discretion even though he was always plotting some stupid deal. Sometimes I wake up at four o'clock in the morning and I can hear someone down there. It might be my mam. She misses him too.

Holly: Don't shoot the messenger lol.

So I tried Holly's birthday. It didn't work. I texted her. Not you anyway.

Holly: LOL didn't expect. Did you get fourteen out?

Me: Nope. Think there's a mistake in the book.

We were talking about Maths.

Our Maths book has like a mistake in every problem. Or every second one. It would go: A normal distribution has mean −x 45 and standard deviation 5. (i) Find the range within which 72% of the distribution lies. (ii) Find the range within which 90% of the distribution lies. (iii) What percentage of the distribution lies within 3 standard deviations of the mean? And the fucking answer to (i) would be outside the given range. Ditto for (ii). It's like it was written by a government economist. One of those guys who is surprised that the arse fell out of the world one fine night when he thought the Celtic Tiger

Would Last Until The Day Of Judgement. It's like our textbook is a prophet of the Armageddon to come. No matter what your numbers tell you, it says, the answer will be a disaster.

I tried Serena's birthday and it worked. The startup sound was like an electric shock. It came alive in my hand. I didn't know what to think. I knew from Maths that in a group of twenty-three (like my class) the probability of two people sharing the same birthday was 50%, but what was it for sharing the same year?

That old iPhone home screen. I knew everything about it. It is designed to warm your heart. There were twenty-seven text messages and forty-one missed calls. The calls were all from one number. I looked at the text messages.

There were eight from the day he died.

Where are you?

Anser FFS im waiting for u at the house

Ur late??!!

Fuck u.

Why dont u anser?

R u ok?

Tell me ur ok

Matt?

I wanted to text back: I'm fucking dead bitch. But I didn't do it. I scrolled back and back. They were mostly making dates.

See you at 7?

Yay

How about 7.15?

CYA then

Delayed at meeting

Fun

I kept going back. Who was it? There was no name. The address book was empty. His Mail didn't link to any email. The stocks app was just the standard stocks. They were all down. The FindPhone was blocked for data. It didn't want to be found. There were no Voice Memos. The App Store was showing seven updates. He never bothered to update anything. There were no Notes. The Calendar was blank. My dad was a bitch Calendar addict. On his business mobile he got alerts about his morning coffee and when it was time to collect his suit from the cleaners and when the rents were due and when a court case was coming up and when he had meetings and when he had golf and when he was having drinks and when Mam's period was due even though she's in early menopause or whatever. On the period days he would always be working late lol. I know the feeling but that option was not available to the rest of us. The Fitness app said he did an average of three thousand steps a day. They say ten thousand is what you need for a healthy heart. Lol. My dad's heart. The steps peaked between five and nine in the evening. The rest of the time he was sitting in the car or in his office. The phone was probably in the envelope. I never saw my dad walk. Maybe the one time he pissed on the Castlemartin project.

The texts had been going on for months. He never cleared any of them. They were all the same. Where are u? or Going to be late. Once or twice she said: I want u. And he'd reply: Me too baby. Or he'd say it and she'd say: I want u 2. How did I know it was a she? If my dad was gay would he have given his life trying to save our family from homosexuality?

So an affair came down to this. Like a bus timetable. Come to Clarinda Park my dear, fuck and go home, cya, ttyl, I want u, me 2. It was pathetic. It was sad. Like we did *Romeo and Juliet*. These violent delights have violent ends, And in their triumph die, like fire and powder which, as they kiss, consume. My fucking life I swear.

What did I think of my dad? I didn't think he had really any interest in human beings. I didn't know whether to be happy or sad. I knew he had a heart because it killed him, but I didn't think it felt anything.

I checked the number in my address book and it wasn't there. It definitely wasn't Serena's number which was a relief. I decided not to tell my mam or Tony but I decided to check Mam's Huawei when she wasn't looking. I put the phone in a drawer and got down to my revision. It was the first properly hot day of May. It was also almost the last day of May. June and exams were like something hard in my belly that I wanted to throw up but it wouldn't come. I would go to university in four months. And then my life would really begin. Even now I felt like a different person idk some sort of different girl to the me that was around for the previous eighteen years more or less. Maybe not having a dad does that to you.

The bitch wasn't on Mam's phone either and she wasn't on Tony's for sure. There were like four girls on Tony's and maybe five hundred men. Definitely some of them were complete strangers, maybe from Grindr or something. But Páraic was the only guy he called. It felt weird to be looking at my brother's life all tied up in a set of telephone numbers that nobody but himself knew anything much about. It was like the iceberg. All that ice below the water. I saw it on a *Titanic* documentary. Except my guess was it was fire for Tony. Since he started seeing Páraic he was even studying. I'd say Páraic would keep his nose to the grindstone. Teachers right?

So I was coming round to the idea that I should ring her up. Except no way she'd answer to a mobile call from a dead man. Like imagine if they accidentally buried the phone with him and he started ass-calling. I don't know if they get a signal down there.

Same difference for texts. Holly wanted me to do it. She thought it was hilarious. She wanted me to to say the thing about Lazarus from 'The Lovesong of J. Alfred Prufrock', the one about coming back from the dead and telling everything. It would probably kill her and I didn't want to kill anyone. If my dad liked her idk maybe I would too, maybe it's genetic. But I wanted to hate her straight up no shit, I wanted that all right. She would be the first person killed by Prufrock. My guess was he wasn't up for it either.

I didn't sleep for a week. Like I'm a bad sleeper anyway. Me sitting on my bed crying. And my mam sitting in Dad's study crying. Three o'clock in the morning at my house.

The day before my exams I phoned her. I couldn't go into a court of law and swear that I recognised the voice. Like do you know that or do you believe it, as the policeman said.

Me: Hello?

Bitch: Hi…?

Me: I'm on my Dad's phone.

Bitch: Oh…

Me: Yeah… so…

Bitch: Yeah…

Me: So… I didn't tell my Mam.

Bitch: Oh…? thanks. I guess…

Me: Ok bye.

And I hung up. I was shaking so much. I had to sit down. I was afraid she would ring back so I powered the phone down. Then I powered it up again and I had to put Serena's birthday in. And there I was again thinking: How did he even know Serena's birthday? I was supposed to be revising but I couldn't get my head around any of it. Tomorrow was English Paper I and there was nothing you could revise for that anyway. I took The Dog for a walk. We went down Regan's Glen, it was my first time

294

back since the purse incident. Followed by the murder incident and all the other incidents. It was dry but there was a low grey cloud. The air was electric. There were bees idk bumble bees maybe, going crazy. It was one of those busy quiet days. I went right down to the river. It's like deep-sea diving. The further down you go the closer you get to silence. Except you hear small things like a bird moving in a brake of briers or a billion bees getting high. And anyway deep sea diving is kinda noisy idk you hear your own bubbles all the time, in the movies anyway. There was a flat stone down there, maybe the start of a bridge one time, or maybe my grandad was thinking of a dam or something. And I sat on it and took my shoes off and put my feet in the water while The Dog went looking for another dead person's purse. The water in that stream looks brown but when you take your feet out they're the same colour as before. It must be an optical illusion. And I started messing with the phone and idk why I never swiped the home screen before but there was a second page and it had WhatsApp and there were photos.

So this is really the history of how I grew up. Or at least the history of how I turned into a History student. I've left out bits. Like the history of how I lost my virginity to a biochemistry second-year. Or the history of how I did my first essay, which was a history of calamity. All the histories. Holly and Serena, Mam and Tony and Tosser and Páraic too.

Serena is in some sort of institution that cures people who need to be cured. Maybe in America. They have a cure for everything over there, even if you're not sick. They're going to need about forty different therapies for Serena, including dinosaur onesies. I asked her Mam if I could write to her and she said the institute was insisting on no outside contact. So that was that.

Holly is doing languages. She is planning an Erasmus already. She's going to Italy. She has fallen in love with one of the Italian lecturers. She has completely changed her image. She dresses like a bitch fashionista from idk maybe Milan. High boots and tight jeans and blouses. The lecturer likes her idk I think they're a couple, which is legit not what I expected. The lecturer dresses the same way except she wears skirts. Holly, of course, speaks

Italian like an Italian after only five months. I don't know how she does it. She like absorbs languages.

Tosser is an actual frigging engineer now. He texted me on John Brown's anniversary. We miss him. And I miss Tony, he's in London working on the next big thing, which is something the internet has every morning at eight o'clock. And Páraic went too. He's teaching in Hackney. Idk if they do Science through Irish there, probs not. And it looks like my mam will hold onto the house. We have declared peace, or at least remorse and regrets, and we miss Dad the way you miss a gale of wind after a long calm spell. He was the noise in our lives after all. But I don't think his tenants miss him, or maybe they do.

And still every night Holly texts me: Best year worst year favourite food? And I text back: 2013 2015 omelette 😊. And Holly replies: Marry me babe. Goodnight sleep tight 😊. Holly and me, still best friends forever. Idk. Maybe.

ABOUT WILLIAM WALL

William Wall was born in Cork, Ireland. He is the author of five previous novels, including *This is the Country*, which was longlisted for the 2005 Man Booker Prize, four collections of poetry and three volumes of short fiction, including *The Islands*, which won the 2017 Drue Heinz Literature Prize, the first European author to do so. He has received many awards and prizes including the Virginia Faulkner Award, the Patrick Kavanagh Award, the Writers' Week/Ireland Fund Poetry Prize, and the Seán Ó Faoláin Prize and he has been short-listed for many others including the Irish Book Awards, the Raymond Carver Prize and the Manchester Fiction Prize. His work has been translated into many languages and he translates from Italian. He holds a PhD from the School of English, University College Cork.